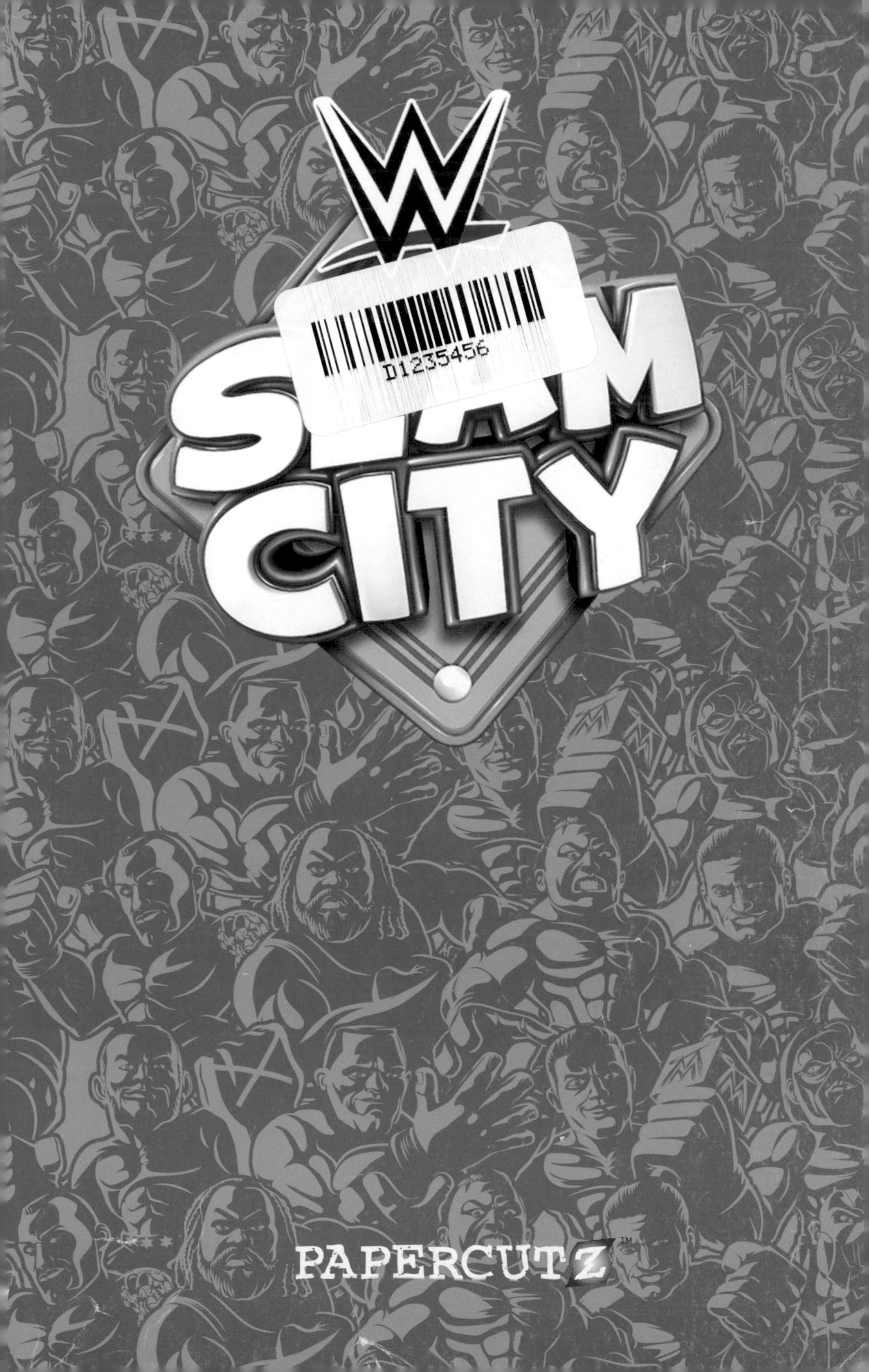
W
SLAM CITY
PAPERCUTZ™

OTHER GREAT GRAPHIC NOVELS AVAILABLE FROM PAPERCUTZ

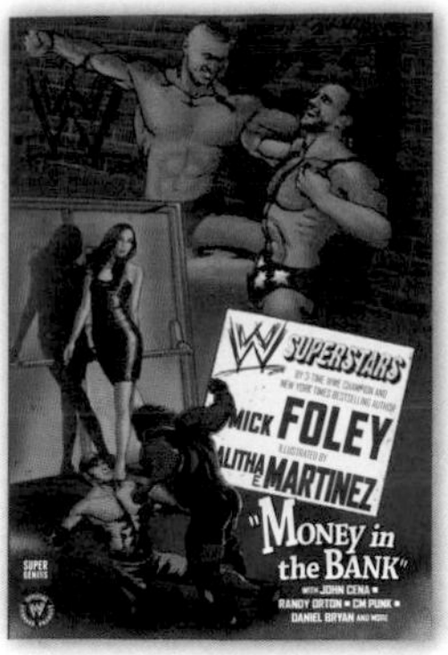
WWE SUPERSTARS
MICK FOLEY
ALITHA MARTINEZ
"Money in the BANK"
WWE SUPERSTARS #1

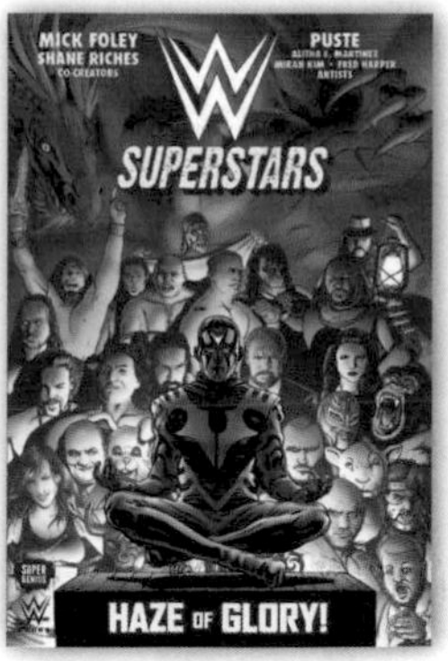
MICK FOLEY
SHANE RICHES
PUSTE
SUPERSTARS
HAZE OF GLORY!
WWE SUPERSTARS #2

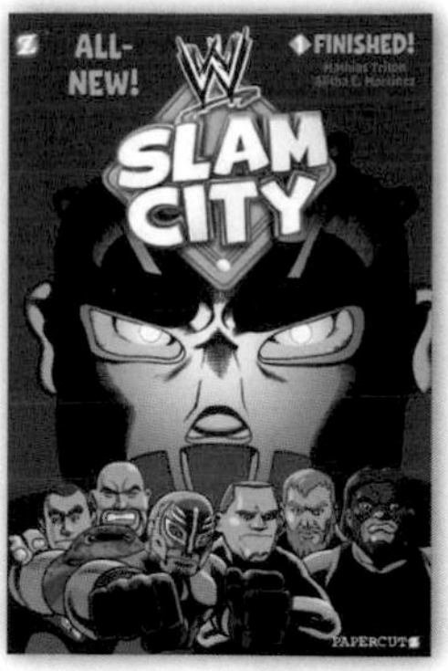
ALL-NEW!
FINISHED!
SLAM CITY
PAPERCUTZ
WWE SLAM CITY #1

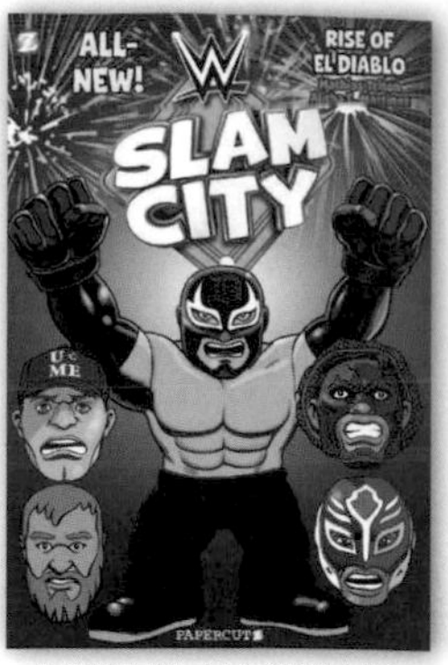
ALL-NEW!
RISE OF EL DIABLO
SLAM CITY
PAPERCUTZ
WWE SLAM CITY #2

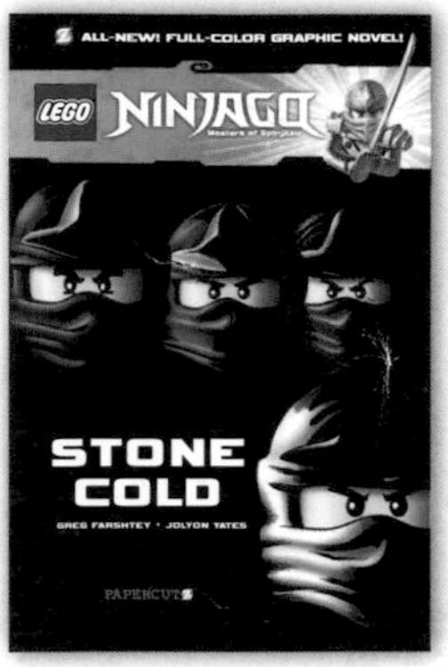
ALL-NEW! FULL-COLOR GRAPHIC NOVEL!
LEGO NINJAGO
STONE COLD
GREG FARSHTEY · JOLYON YATES
PAPERCUTZ
LEGO® NINJAGO #7

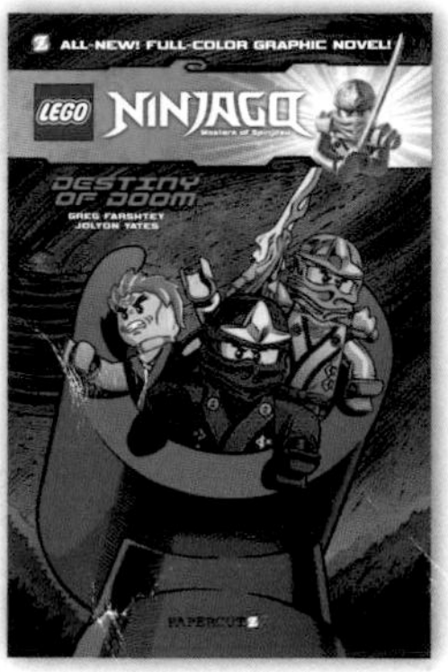
ALL-NEW! FULL-COLOR GRAPHIC NOVEL!
LEGO NINJAGO
DESTINY OF DOOM
GREG FARSHTEY
JOLYON YATES
PAPERCUTZ
LEGO® NINJAGO #8

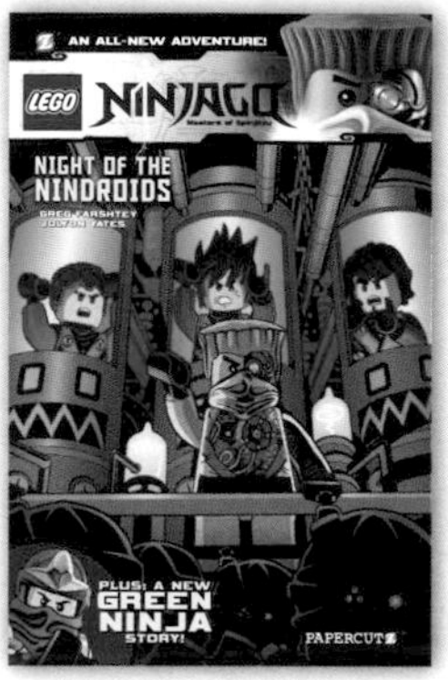
AN ALL-NEW ADVENTURE!
LEGO NINJAGO
NIGHT OF THE NINDROIDS
PLUS: A NEW GREEN NINJA STORY!
PAPERCUTZ
LEGO® NINJAGO #9

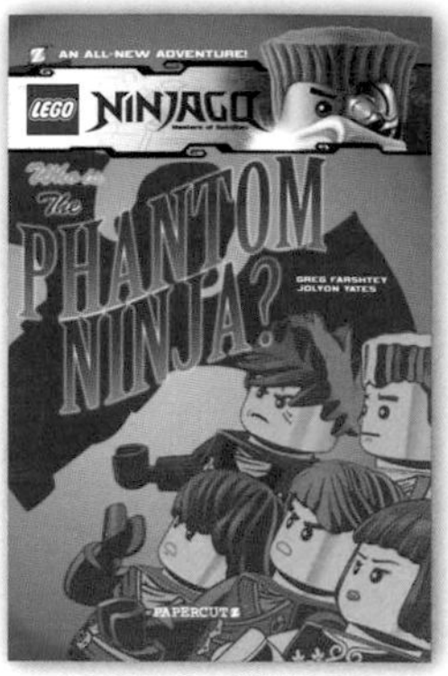
AN ALL-NEW ADVENTURE!
LEGO NINJAGO
Who is The PHANTOM NINJA?
PAPERCUTZ
LEGO® NINJAGO #10

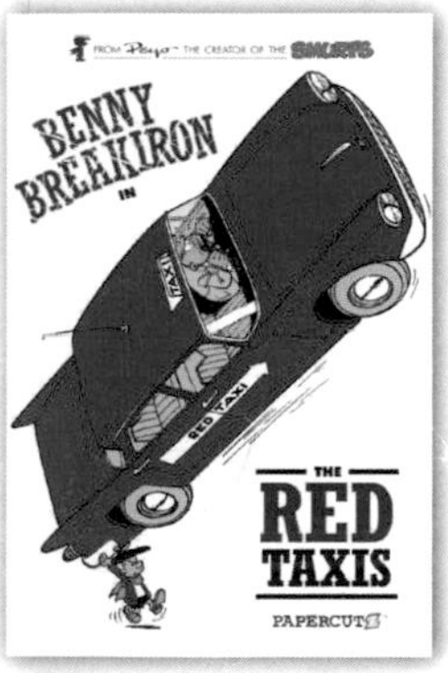
BENNY BREAKIRON
IN
THE RED TAXIS
PAPERCUTZ
BENNY BREAKIRON #1

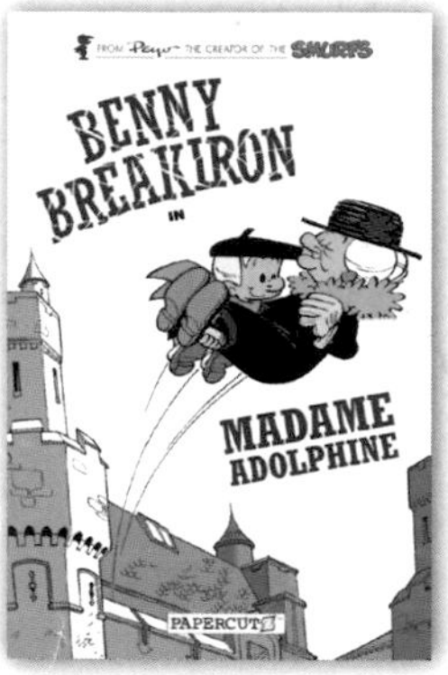
BENNY BREAKIRON
IN
MADAME ADOLPHINE
PAPERCUTZ
BENNY BREAKIRON #2

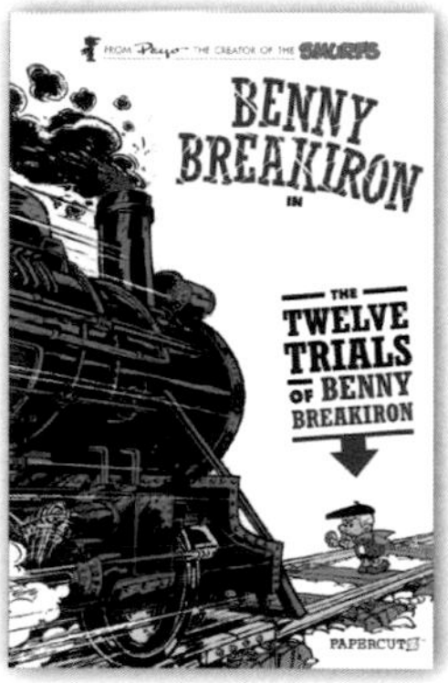
BENNY BREAKIRON
IN
THE TWELVE TRIALS OF BENNY BREAKIRON
PAPERCUTZ
BENNY BREAKIRON #3

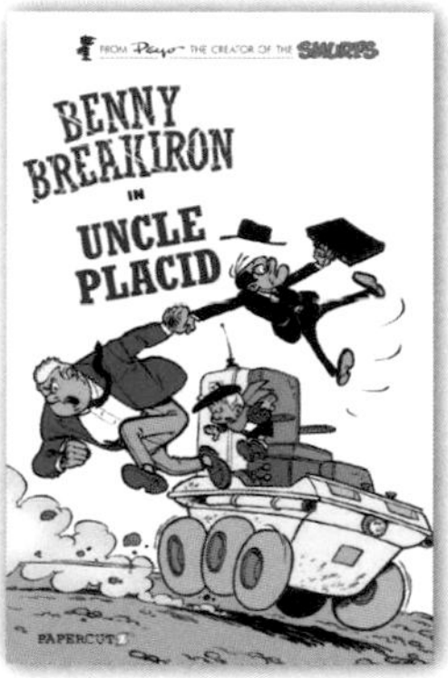
BENNY BREAKIRON
IN
UNCLE PLACID
PAPERCUTZ
BENNY BREAKIRON #4

WWE SUPERSTARS #1 is $9.99 in paperback only; WWE SUPERSTARS #2 is $12.99 in paperback only; WWE SLAM CITY is $7.99 in paperback and $12.99 in hardcover; LEGO NINJAGO is $6.99 each in paperback and $10.99 each in hardcover; and BENNY BREAKIRON is $11.99 each in hardcover only, at booksellers everywhere. You can also order online at papercutz.com. Or call 1-800-886-1223, Monday through Friday, 9 – 5 EST. MC, Visa, and AmEx accepted. To order by mail, please add $4.00 for postage and handling for first book ordered, $1.00 for each additional book and make check payable to NBM Publishing. Send to: Papercutz, 160 Broadway, Suite 700, East Wing, New York, NY 10038

Papercutz graphic novels are also available digitally wherever e-books are sold.

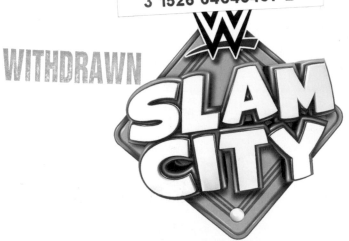

#2 "RISE OF EL DIABLO"

Mathias Triton – Writer

Alitha E. Martinez – Artist

JayJay Jackson – Colorist

PAPERCUTZ™

New York

PREVIOUSLY IN WWE SLAM CITY: The mysterious **Finisher** has fired all the **WWE Superstars** from the ring to Slam City to find real jobs. John Cena fixes cars at Greasy Lube, Rey Mysterio is a crossing guard and Kane is the lunch server at Slam City Elementary school...

WWE SLAM CITY
#2 "Rise of El Diablo"

Mathias Triton – Writer
Alitha E. Martinez – Artist
Jolyon Yates – Cover Artist
JayJay Jackson – Colorist
Tom Orzechowski – Letterer
Noah Sharma – Editorial Intern
Jeff Whitman – Production Coordinator
Michael Petranek – Associate Editor
Eric Lyga, Steven Pantaleo – Special Thanks

Jim Salicrup
Editor-in-Chief

ISBN: 978-1-62991-066-6 paperback edition
ISBN: 978-1-62991-067-3 hardcover edition

Papercutz books may be purchased for business or promotional use. For information on bulk purchases please contact Macmillan Corporate and Premium Sales Department at (800) 221-7945 x5442.

Printed in China
February 2015 by OG Printing, LTD
Units 2&3, 5/F, Lemmi Centre
50 Hoi Yuen Road
Kwong Tong, Kowloon

Distributed by Macmillan
First Printing

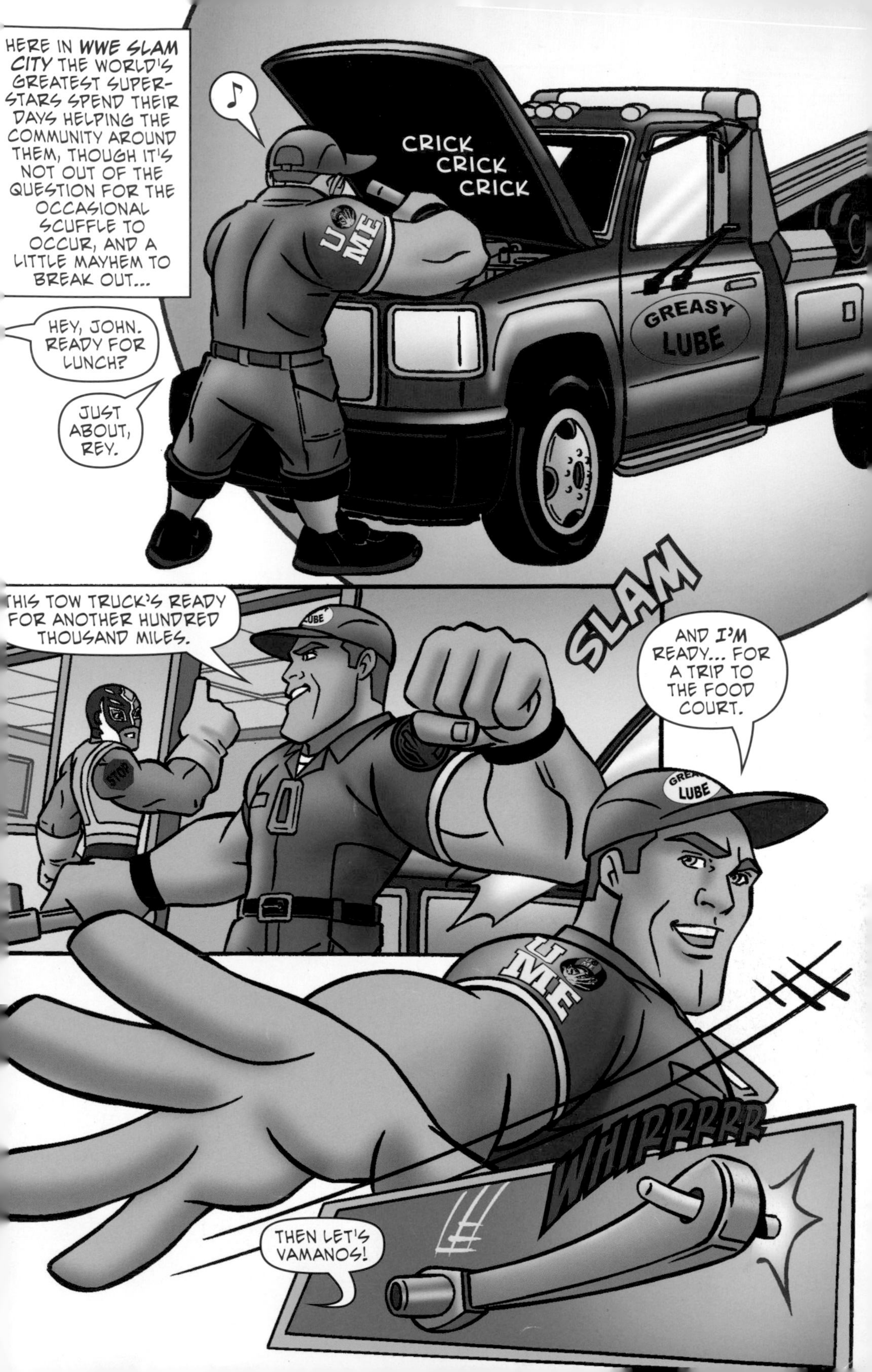

HERE IN **WWE SLAM CITY** THE WORLD'S GREATEST SUPER-STARS SPEND THEIR DAYS HELPING THE COMMUNITY AROUND THEM, THOUGH IT'S NOT OUT OF THE QUESTION FOR THE OCCASIONAL SCUFFLE TO OCCUR, AND A LITTLE MAYHEM TO BREAK OUT...
♪
CRICK CRICK CRICK
GREASY LUBE
HEY, JOHN. READY FOR LUNCH?
JUST ABOUT, REY.
SLAM
THIS TOW TRUCK'S READY FOR ANOTHER HUNDRED THOUSAND MILES.
AND I'M READY... FOR A TRIP TO THE FOOD COURT.
WHIRRRRR
THEN LET'S VAMANOS!

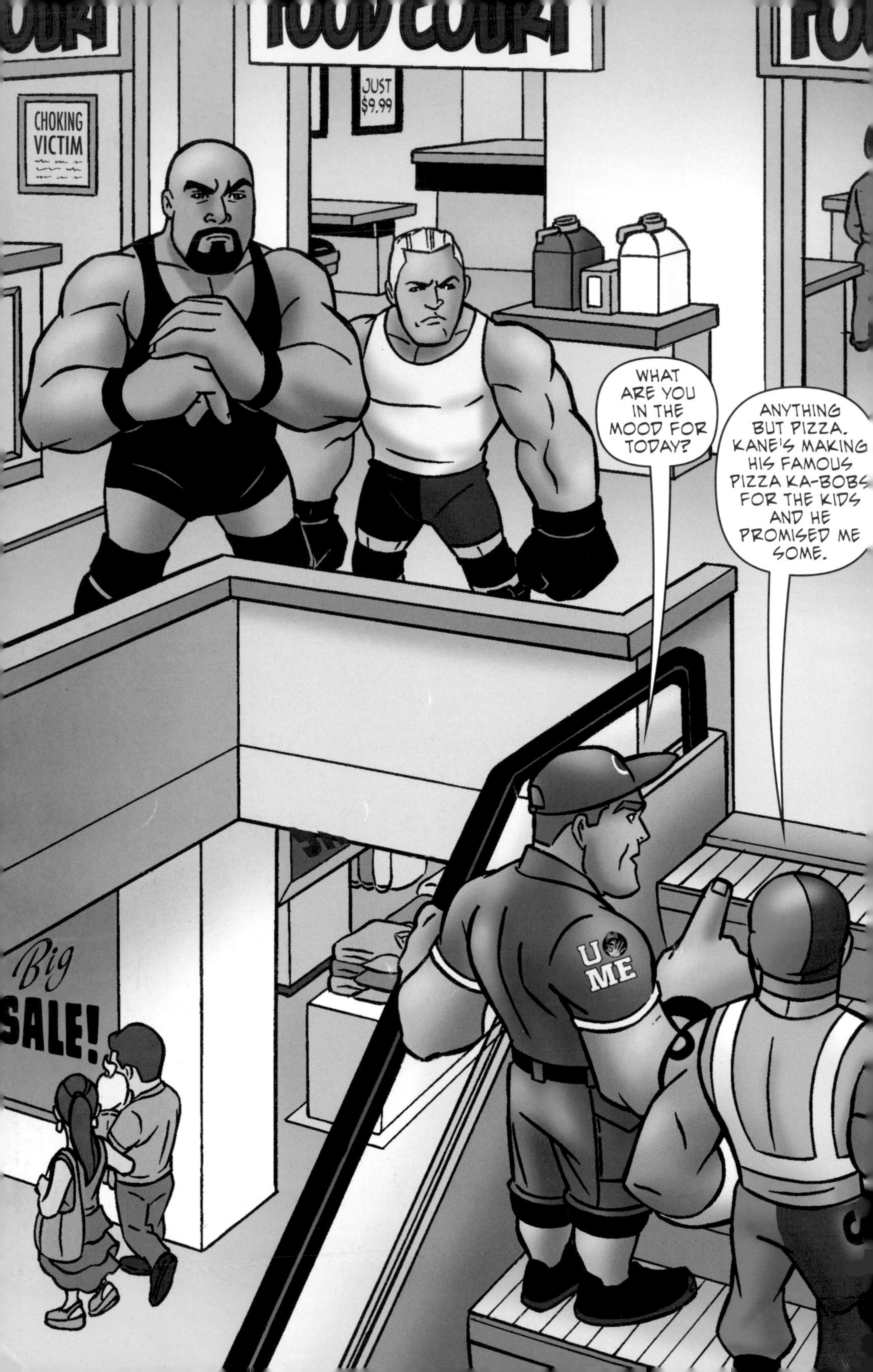
FOOD COURT
JUST $9.99
CHOKING VICTIM
WHAT ARE YOU IN THE MOOD FOR TODAY?
ANYTHING BUT PIZZA. KANE'S MAKING HIS FAMOUS PIZZA KA-BOBS FOR THE KIDS AND HE PROMISED ME SOME.
U C ME
Big SALE!

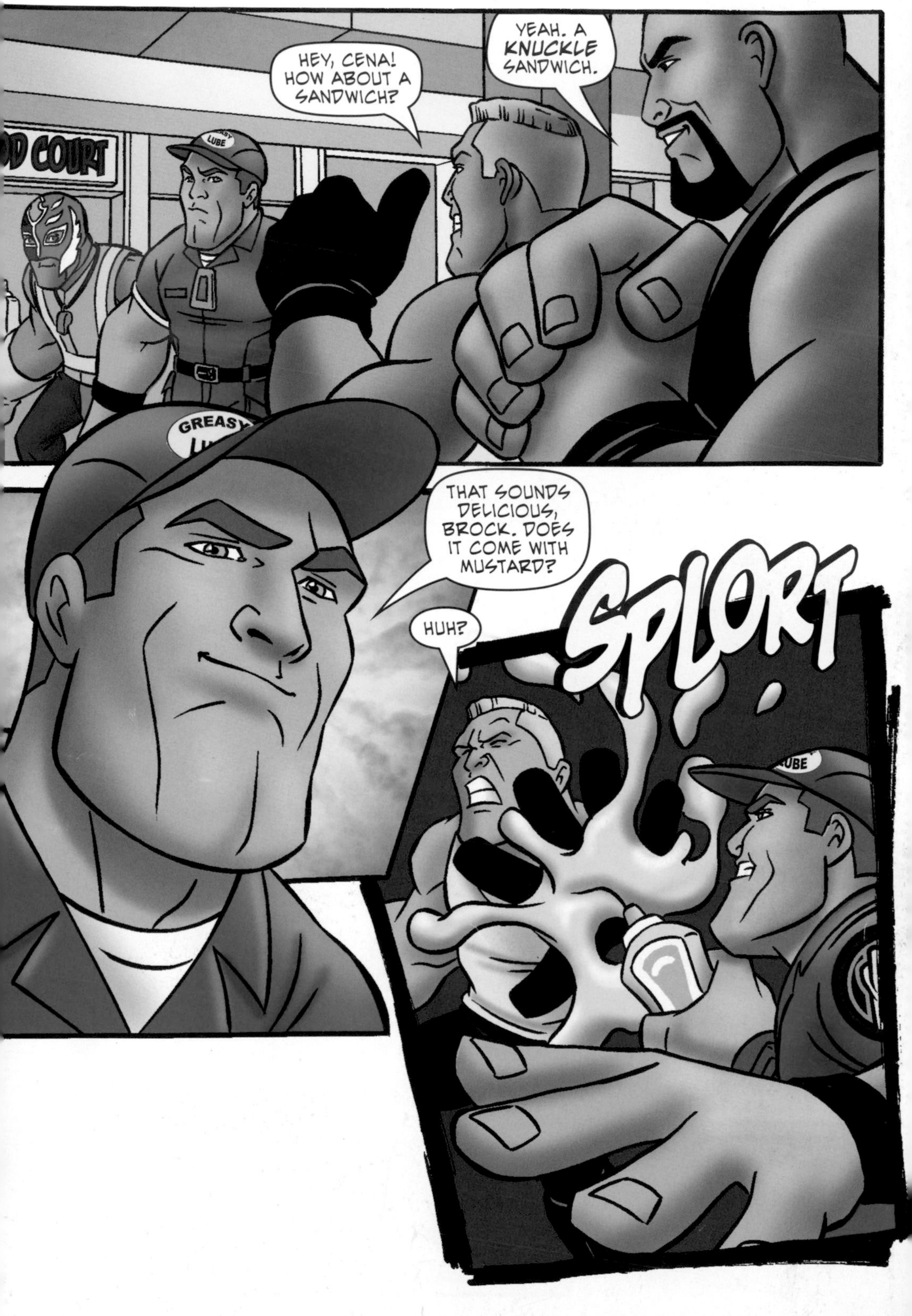

HEY, CENA! HOW ABOUT A SANDWICH?
YEAH. A KNUCKLE SANDWICH.
FOOD COURT
GREASY LUBE
THAT SOUNDS DELICIOUS, BROCK. DOES IT COME WITH MUSTARD?
HUH?
SPLORT

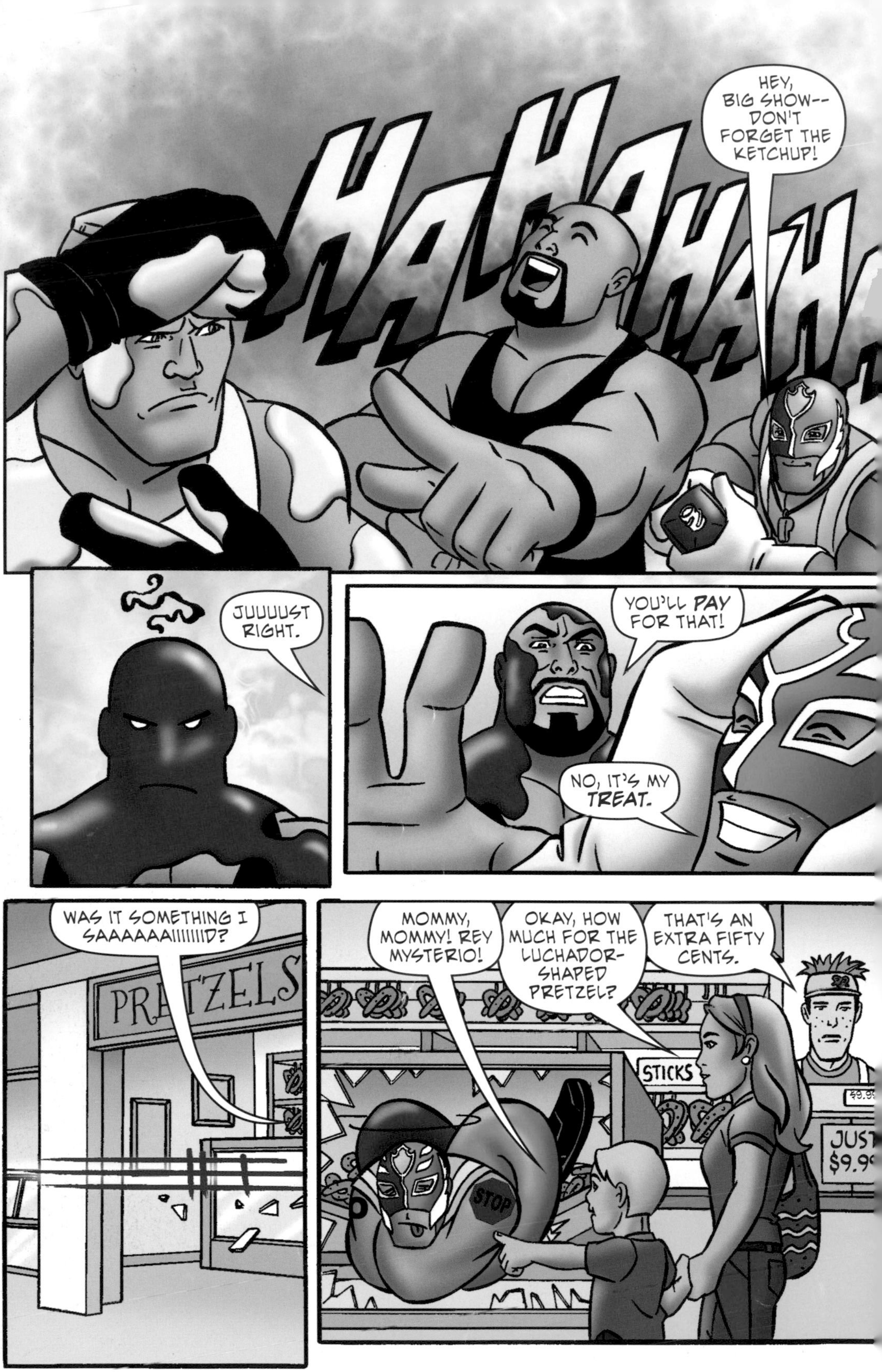
HAHAHAHAH...
HEY, BIG SHOW-- DON'T FORGET THE KETCHUP!
JUUUUST RIGHT.
YOU'LL PAY FOR THAT!
NO, IT'S MY TREAT.
WAS IT SOMETHING I SAAAAAAIIIIIIID?
PRETZELS
MOMMY, MOMMY! REY MYSTERIO!
OKAY, HOW MUCH FOR THE LUCHADOR-SHAPED PRETZEL?
THAT'S AN EXTRA FIFTY CENTS.
STICKS
STOP

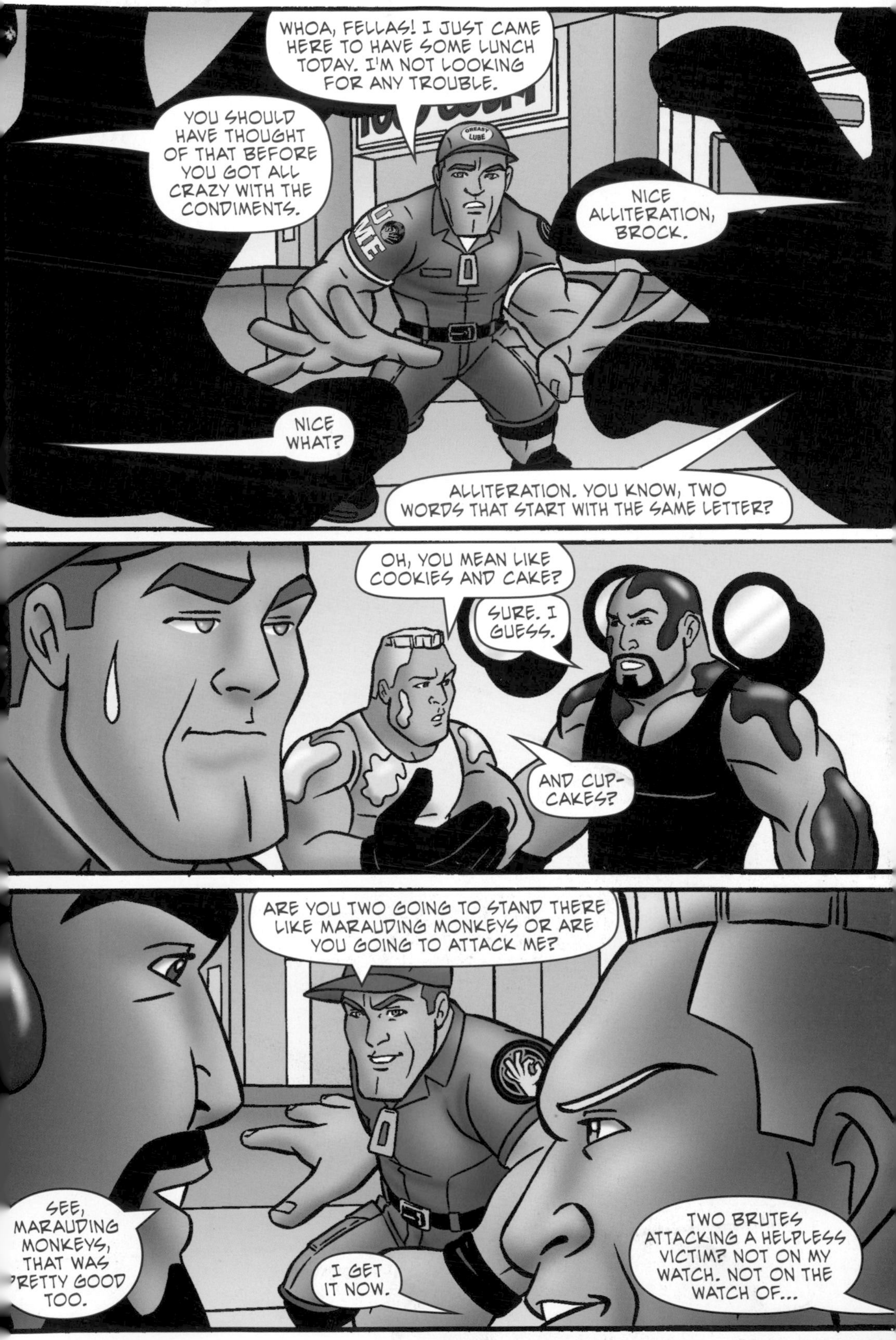
WHOA, FELLAS! I JUST CAME HERE TO HAVE SOME LUNCH TODAY. I'M NOT LOOKING FOR ANY TROUBLE.
YOU SHOULD HAVE THOUGHT OF THAT BEFORE YOU GOT ALL CRAZY WITH THE CONDIMENTS.
NICE ALLITERATION, BROCK.
NICE WHAT?
ALLITERATION. YOU KNOW, TWO WORDS THAT START WITH THE SAME LETTER?
OH, YOU MEAN LIKE COOKIES AND CAKE?
SURE. I GUESS.
AND CUP-CAKES?
ARE YOU TWO GOING TO STAND THERE LIKE MARAUDING MONKEYS OR ARE YOU GOING TO ATTACK ME?
SEE, MARAUDING MONKEYS, THAT WAS PRETTY GOOD TOO.
I GET IT NOW.
TWO BRUTES ATTACKING A HELPLESS VICTIM? NOT ON MY WATCH. NOT ON THE WATCH OF...

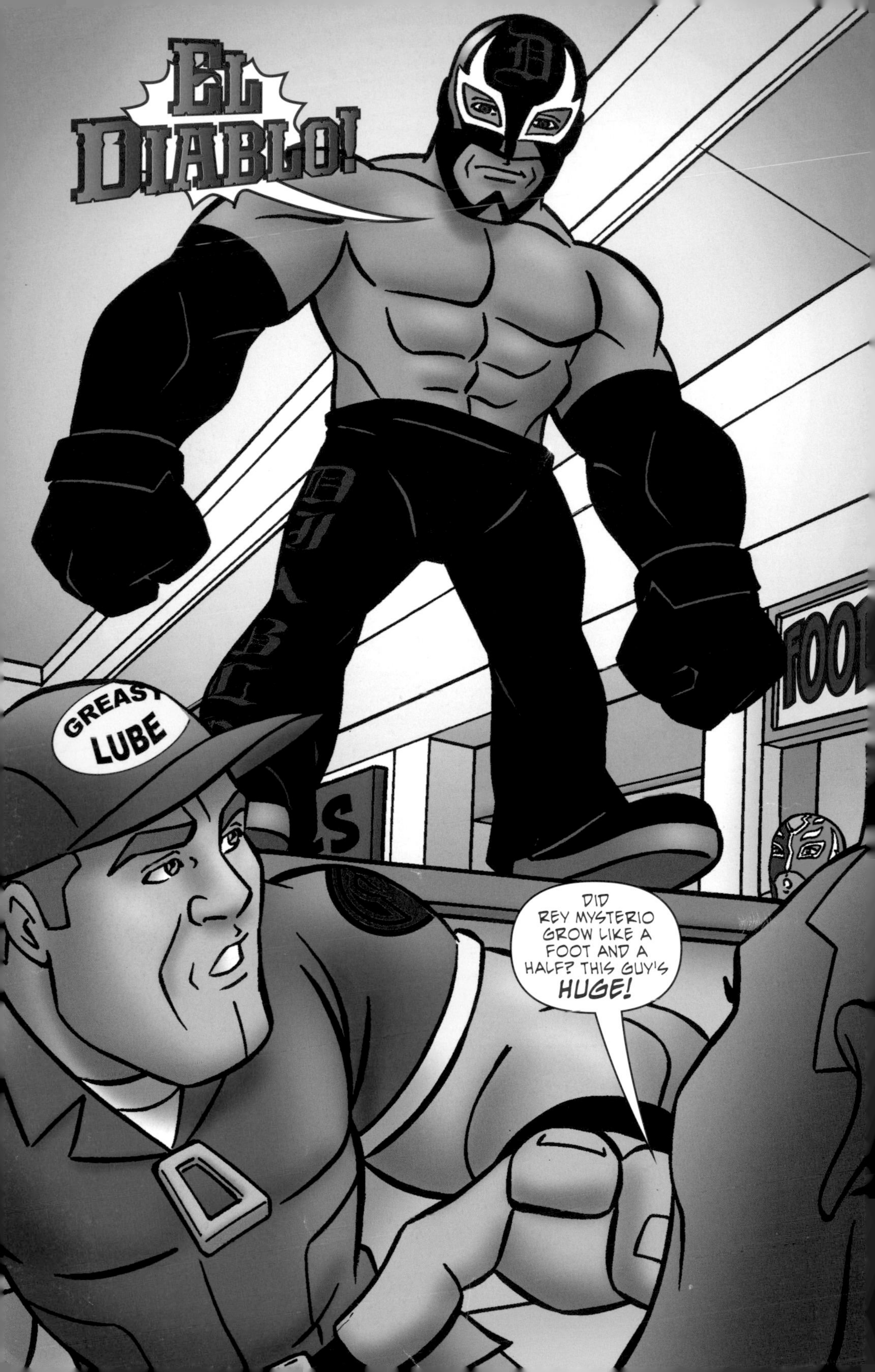
EL DIABLO!
DID REY MYSTERIO GROW LIKE A FOOT AND A HALF? THIS GUY'S HUGE!
GREASY LUBE
FOOD

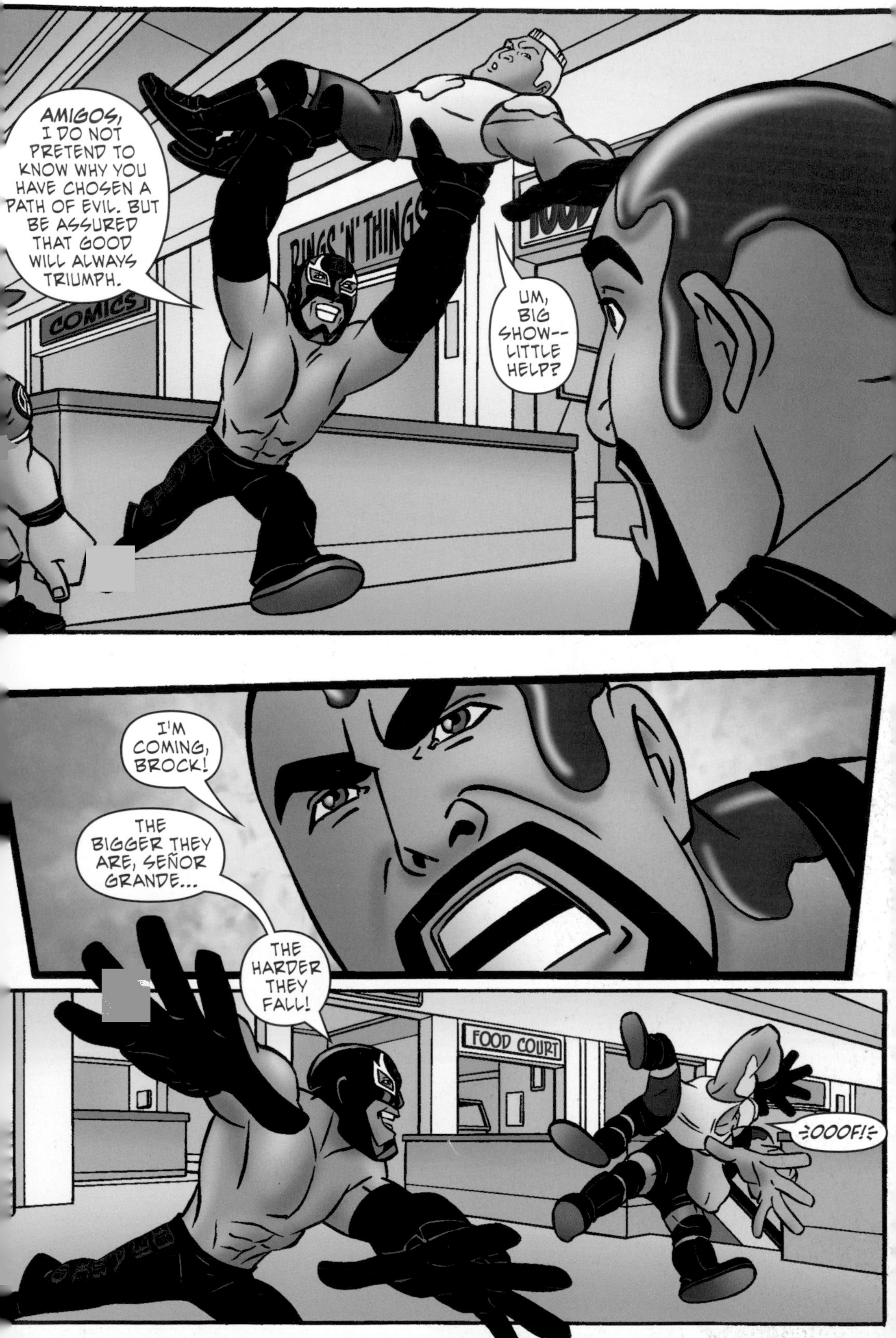
AMIGOS, I DO NOT PRETEND TO KNOW WHY YOU HAVE CHOSEN A PATH OF EVIL. BUT BE ASSURED THAT GOOD WILL ALWAYS TRIUMPH.
COMICS
RINGS 'N' THINGS
UM, BIG SHOW-- LITTLE HELP?
I'M COMING, BROCK!
THE BIGGER THEY ARE, SEÑOR GRANDE...
THE HARDER THEY FALL!
FOOD COURT
OOOF!

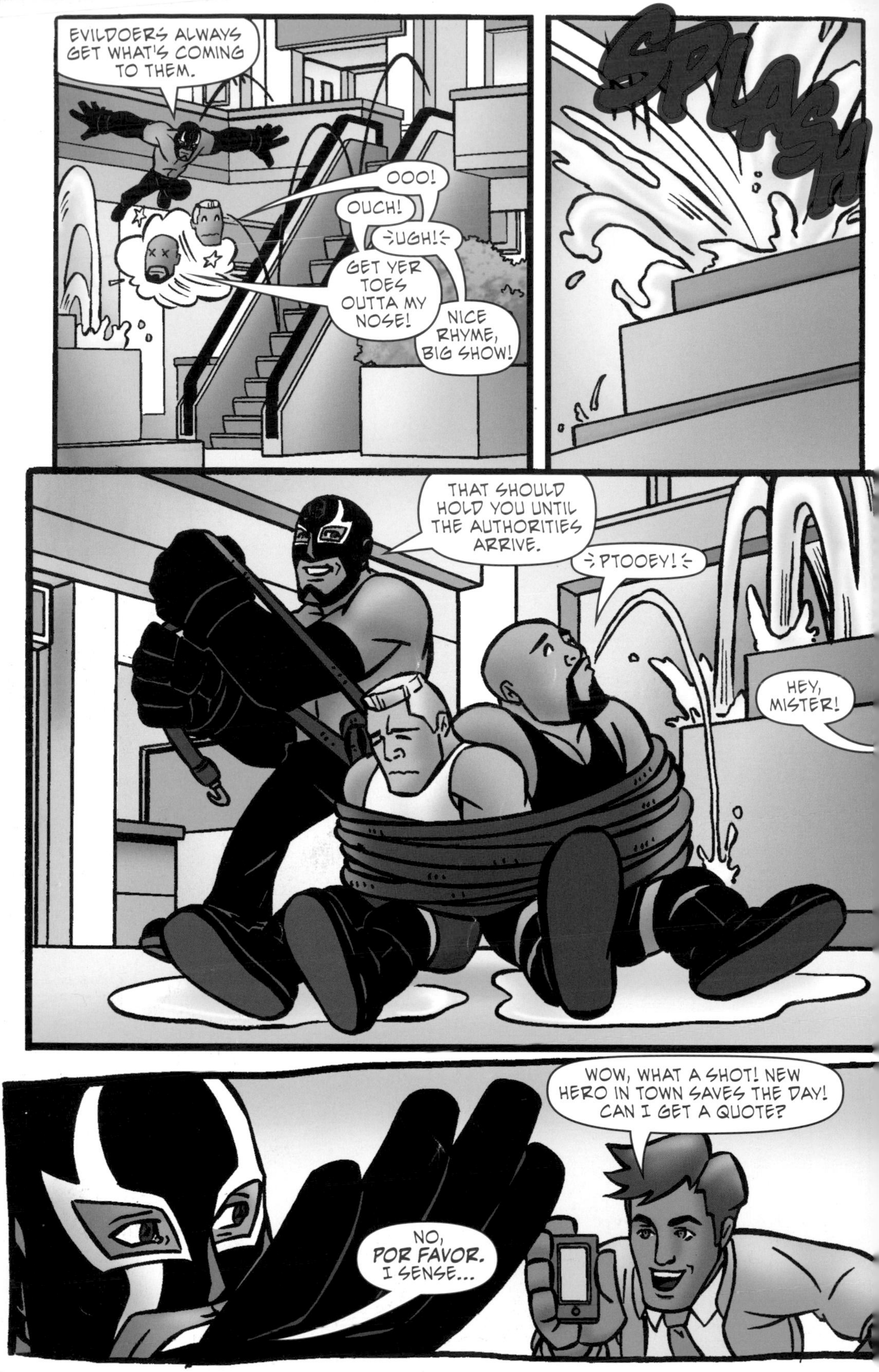
EVILDOERS ALWAYS GET WHAT'S COMING TO THEM.
OOO!
OUCH!
UGH!
GET YER TOES OUTTA MY NOSE!
NICE RHYME, BIG SHOW!
SPLASH
THAT SHOULD HOLD YOU UNTIL THE AUTHORITIES ARRIVE.
PTOOEY!
HEY, MISTER!
WOW, WHAT A SHOT! NEW HERO IN TOWN SAVES THE DAY! CAN I GET A QUOTE?
NO, POR FAVOR. I SENSE...

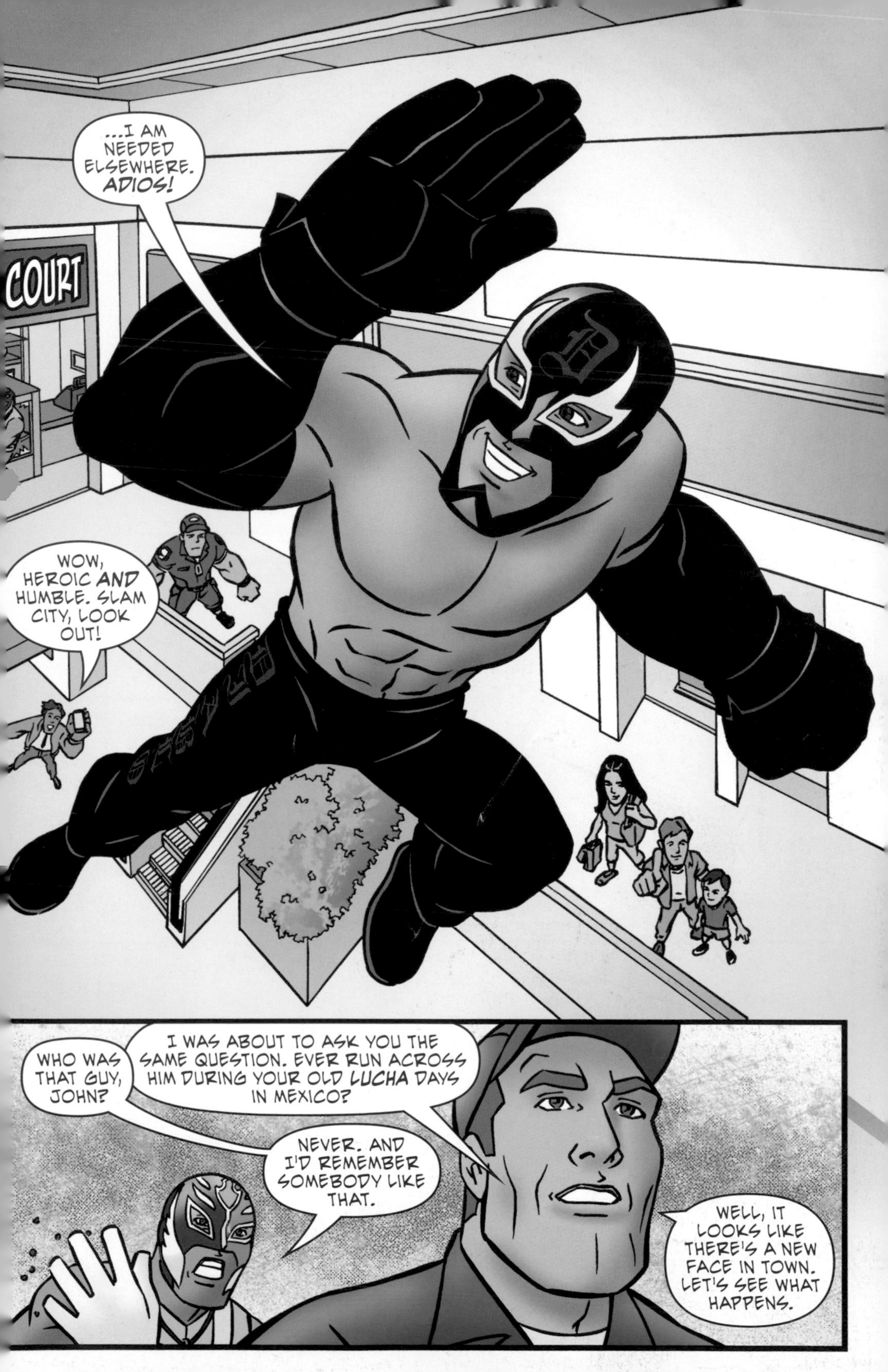

...I AM NEEDED ELSEWHERE. ADIOS!
COURT
WOW, HEROIC AND HUMBLE. SLAM CITY, LOOK OUT!
WHO WAS THAT GUY, JOHN?
I WAS ABOUT TO ASK YOU THE SAME QUESTION. EVER RUN ACROSS HIM DURING YOUR OLD LUCHA DAYS IN MEXICO?
NEVER. AND I'D REMEMBER SOMEBODY LIKE THAT.
WELL, IT LOOKS LIKE THERE'S A NEW FACE IN TOWN. LET'S SEE WHAT HAPPENS.

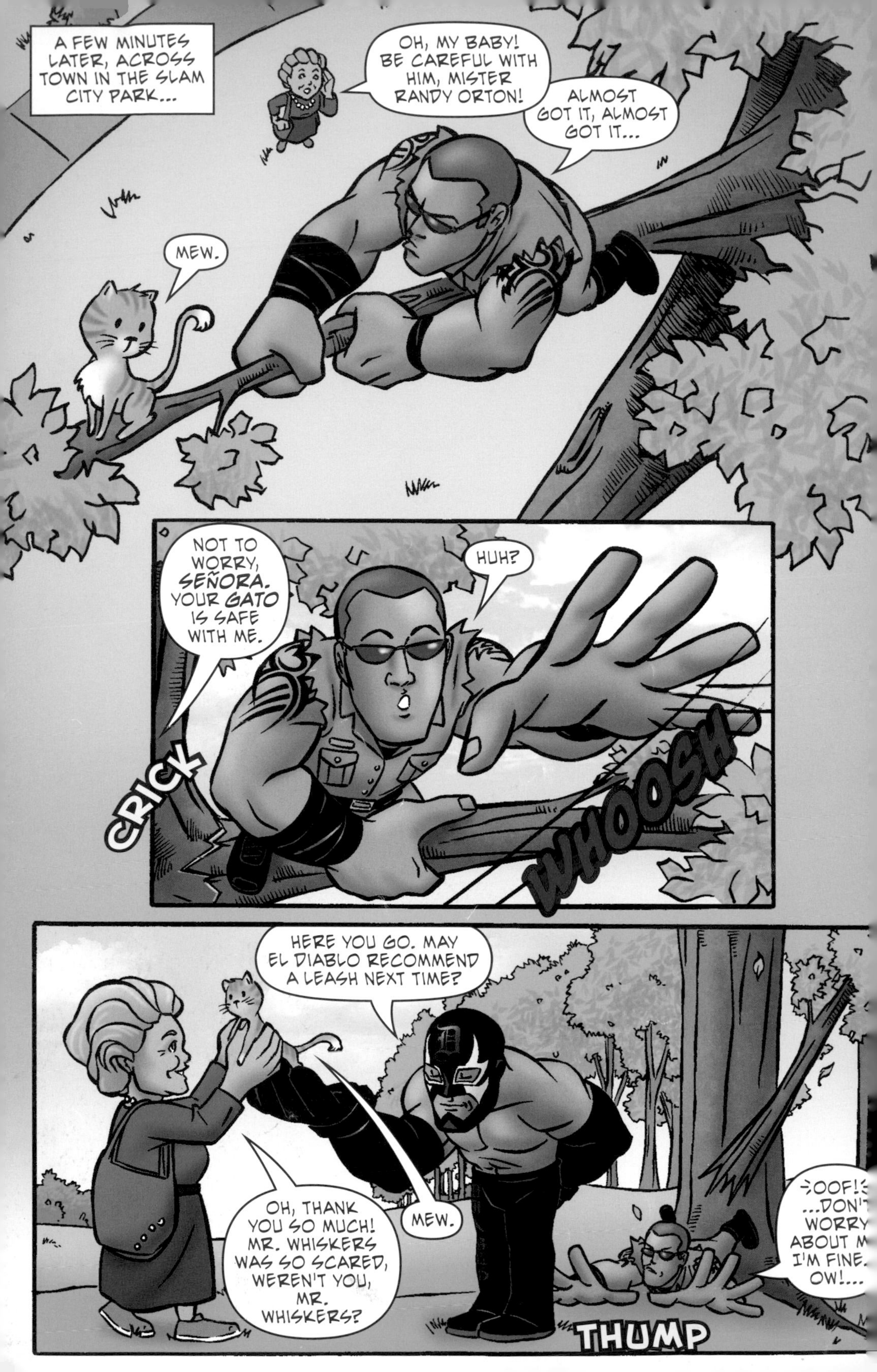
A FEW MINUTES LATER, ACROSS TOWN IN THE SLAM CITY PARK...
OH, MY BABY! BE CAREFUL WITH HIM, MISTER RANDY ORTON!
ALMOST GOT IT, ALMOST GOT IT...
MEW.
NOT TO WORRY, SEÑORA. YOUR GATO IS SAFE WITH ME.
HUH?
CRICK
WHOOSH
HERE YOU GO. MAY EL DIABLO RECOMMEND A LEASH NEXT TIME?
OH, THANK YOU SO MUCH! MR. WHISKERS WAS SO SCARED, WEREN'T YOU, MR. WHISKERS?
MEW.
OOF! ...DON'T WORRY ABOUT M I'M FINE. OW!...
THUMP

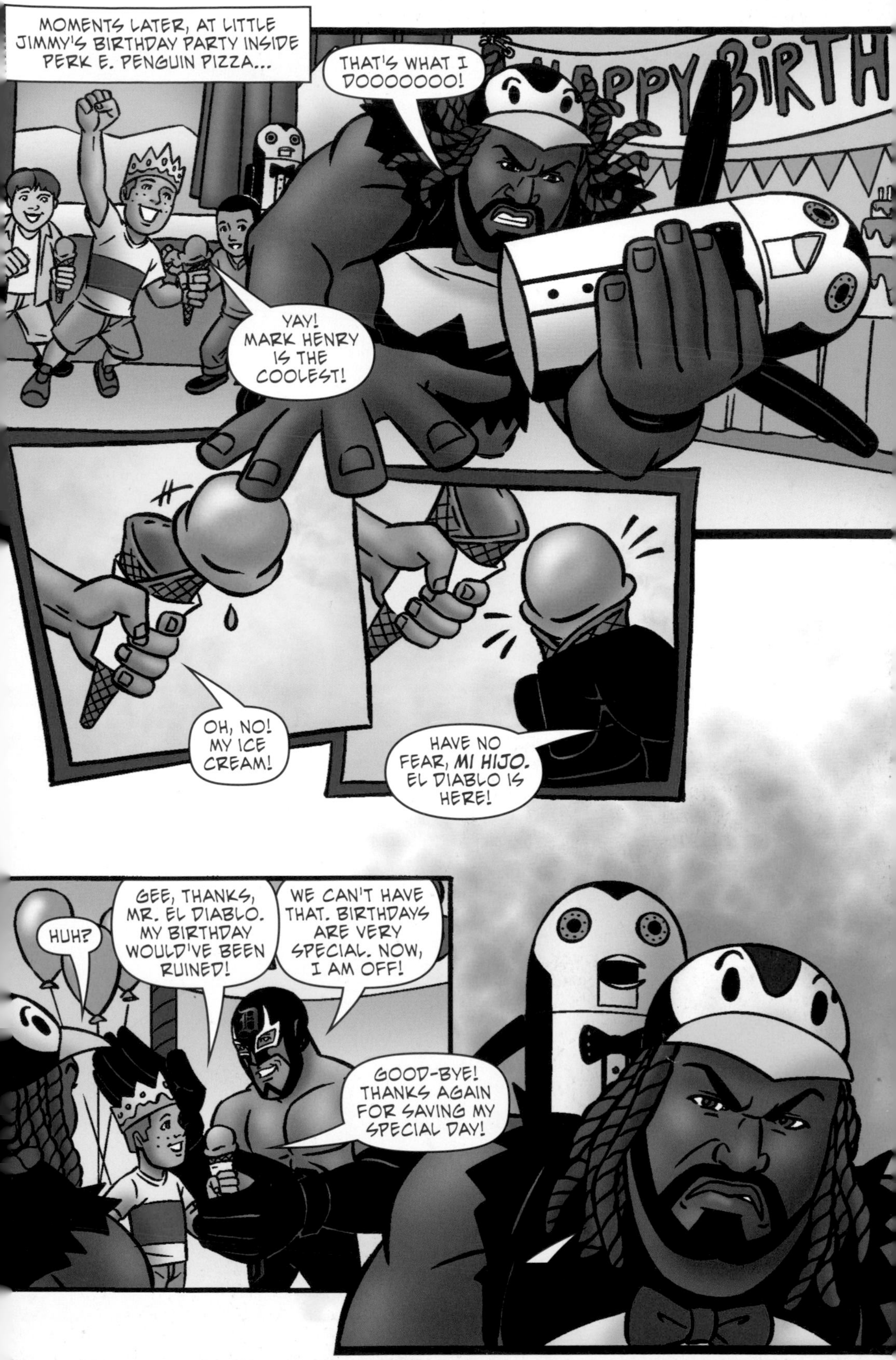
MOMENTS LATER, AT LITTLE JIMMY'S BIRTHDAY PARTY INSIDE PERK E. PENGUIN PIZZA...
THAT'S WHAT I DOOOOOOO!
YAY! MARK HENRY IS THE COOLEST!
OH, NO! MY ICE CREAM!
HAVE NO FEAR, ***MI HIJO.*** EL DIABLO IS HERE!
HUH?
GEE, THANKS, MR. EL DIABLO. MY BIRTHDAY WOULD'VE BEEN RUINED!
WE CAN'T HAVE THAT. BIRTHDAYS ARE VERY SPECIAL. NOW, I AM OFF!
GOOD-BYE! THANKS AGAIN FOR SAVING MY SPECIAL DAY!

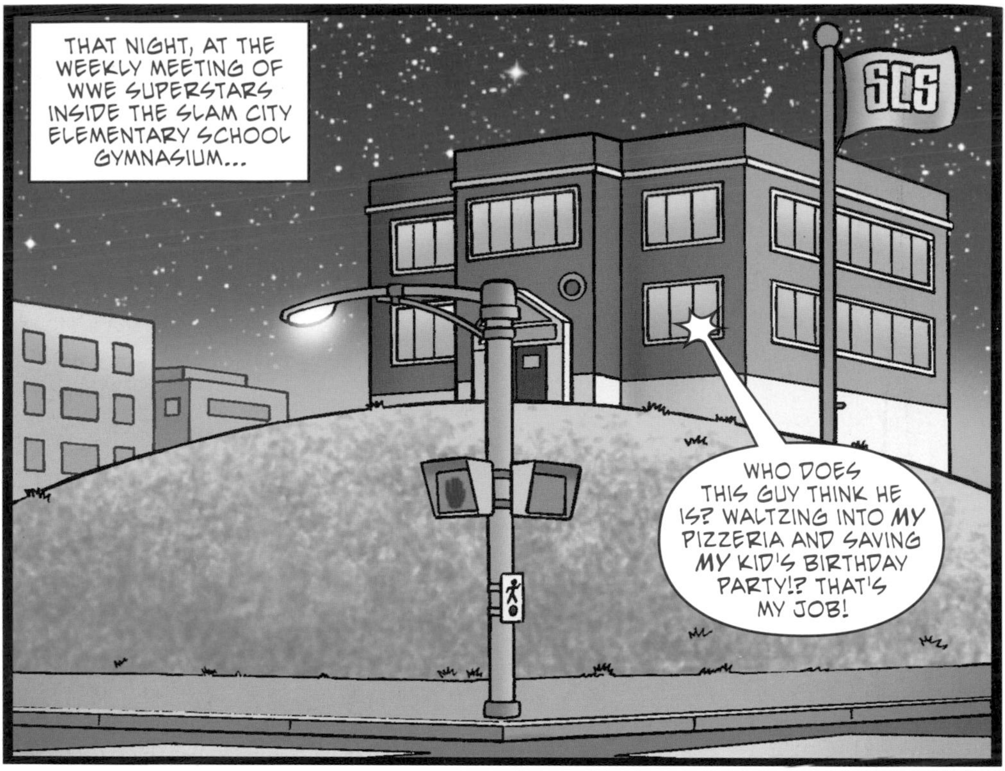
THAT NIGHT, AT THE WEEKLY MEETING OF WWE SUPERSTARS INSIDE THE SLAM CITY ELEMENTARY SCHOOL GYMNASIUM...
SCS
WHO DOES THIS GUY THINK HE IS? WALTZING INTO MY PIZZERIA AND SAVING MY KID'S BIRTHDAY PARTY!? THAT'S MY JOB!

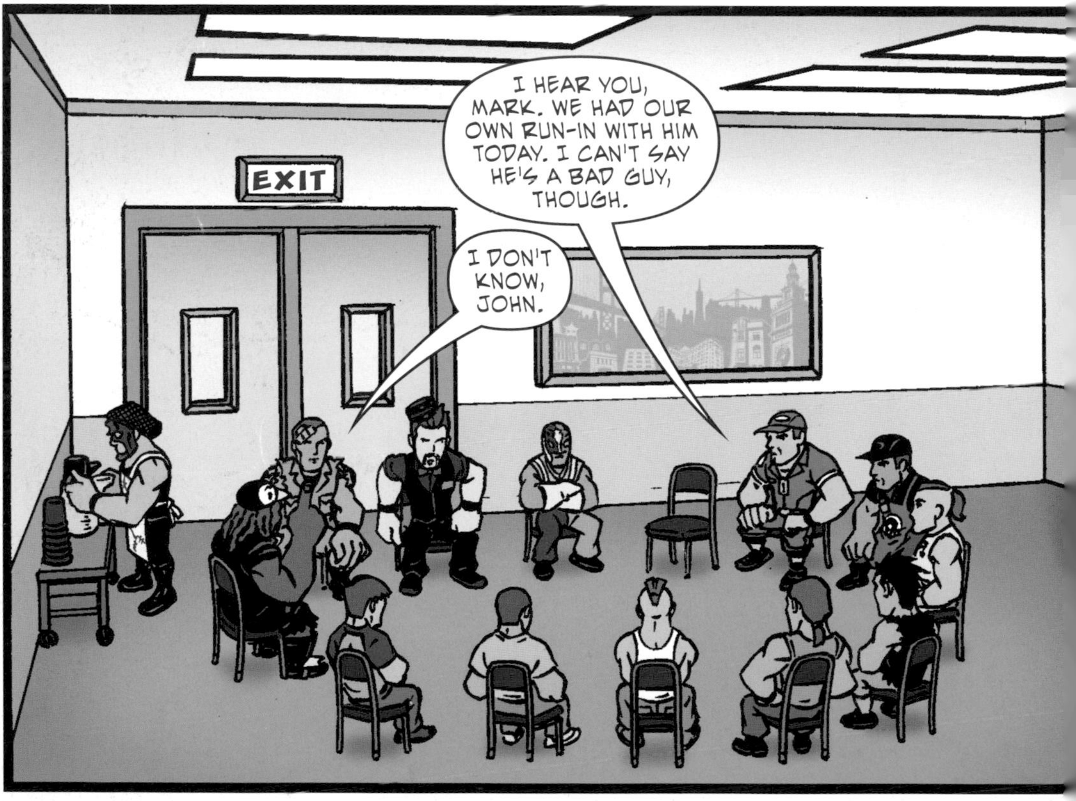
EXIT
I HEAR YOU, MARK. WE HAD OUR OWN RUN-IN WITH HIM TODAY. I CAN'T SAY HE'S A BAD GUY, THOUGH.
I DON'T KNOW, JOHN.

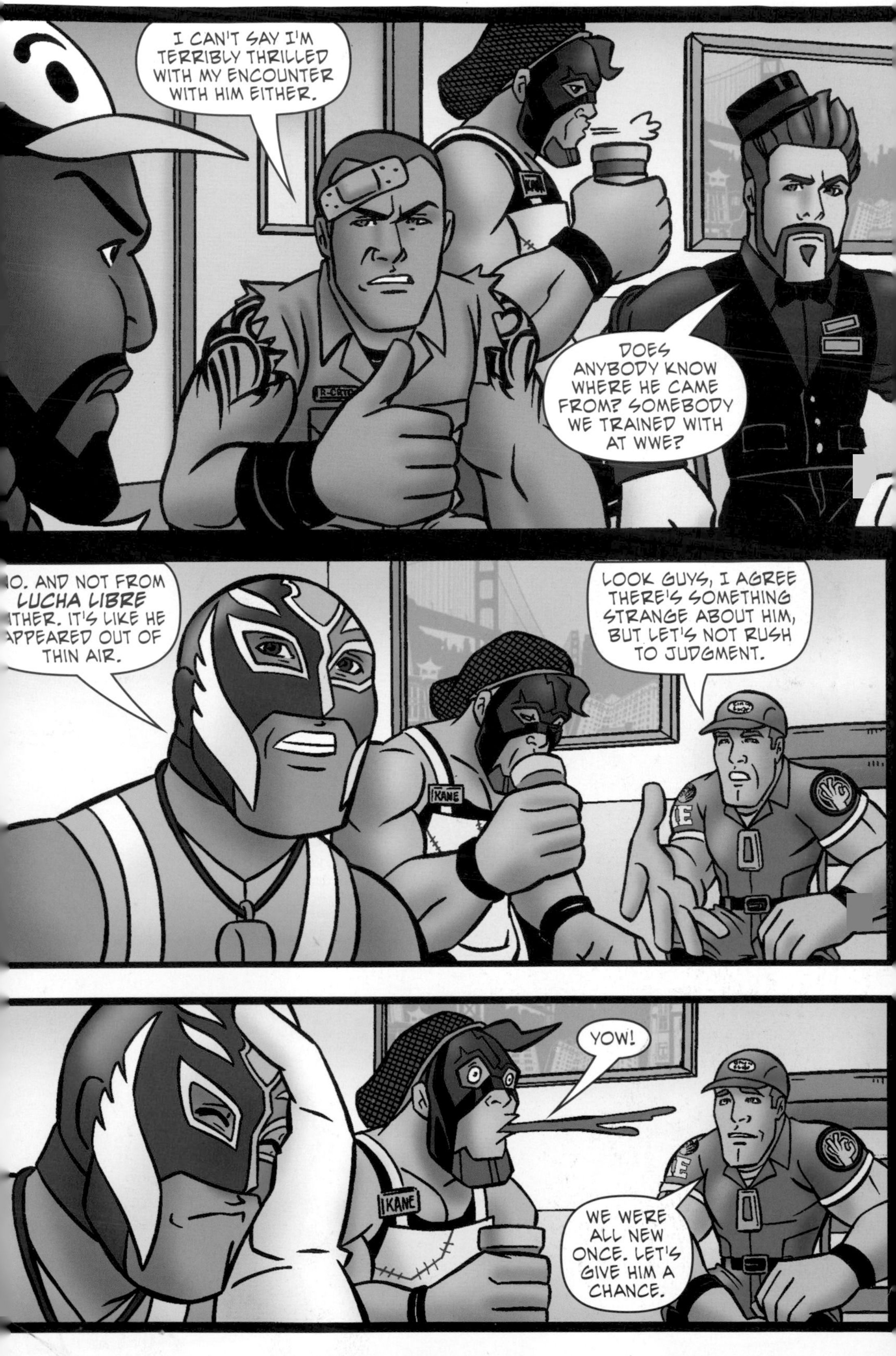
I CAN'T SAY I'M TERRIBLY THRILLED WITH MY ENCOUNTER WITH HIM EITHER.
DOES ANYBODY KNOW WHERE HE CAME FROM? SOMEBODY WE TRAINED WITH AT WWE?
O. AND NOT FROM *LUCHA LIBRE* ITHER. IT'S LIKE HE PPEARED OUT OF THIN AIR.
LOOK GUYS, I AGREE THERE'S SOMETHING STRANGE ABOUT HIM, BUT LET'S NOT RUSH TO JUDGMENT.
YOW!
WE WERE ALL NEW ONCE. LET'S GIVE HIM A CHANCE.

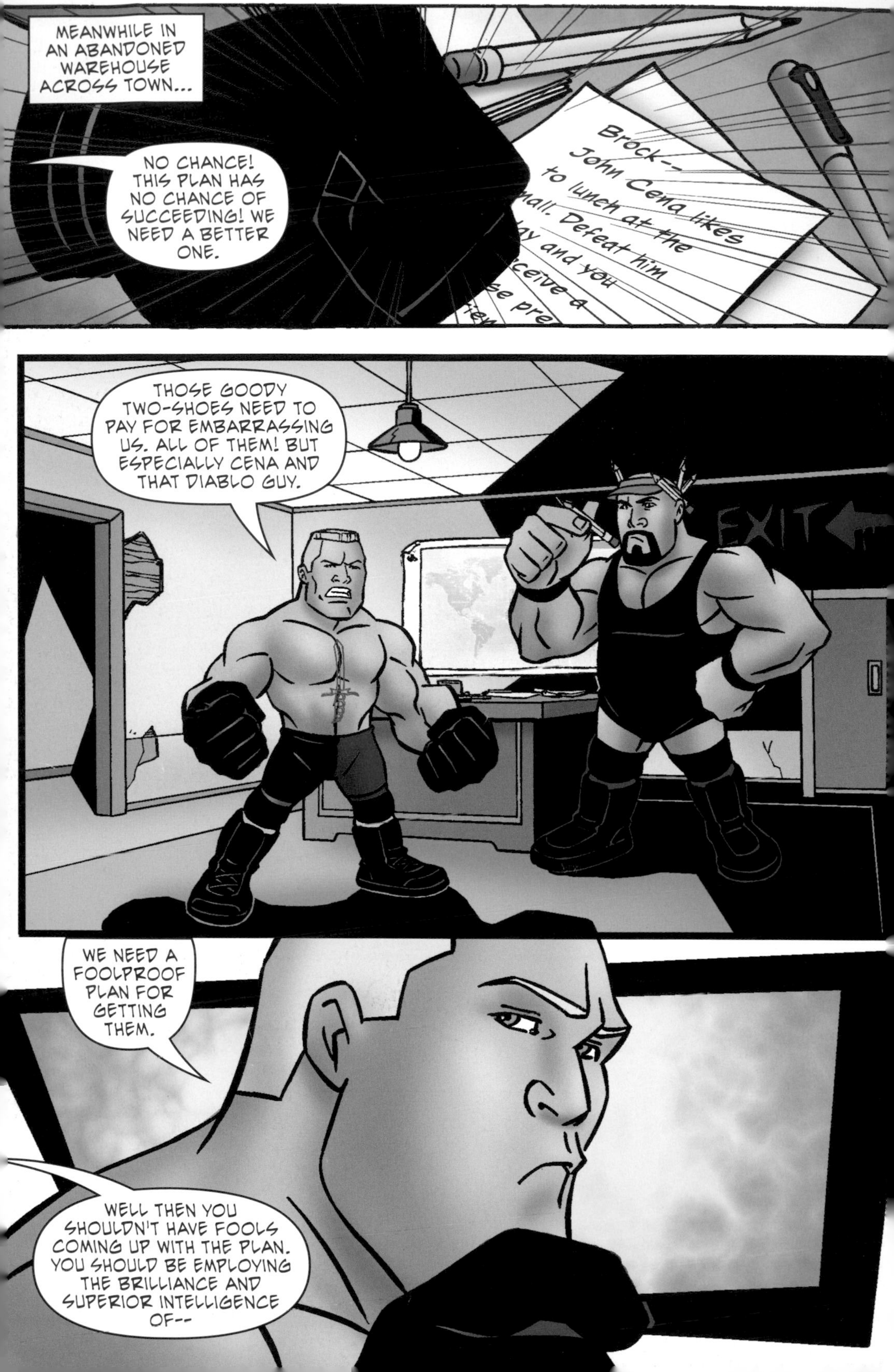
MEANWHILE IN AN ABANDONED WAREHOUSE ACROSS TOWN...
NO CHANCE! THIS PLAN HAS NO CHANCE OF SUCCEEDING! WE NEED A BETTER ONE.
Brock--
John Cena likes
to lunch at the
Defeat him
THOSE GOODY TWO-SHOES NEED TO PAY FOR EMBARRASSING US. ALL OF THEM! BUT ESPECIALLY CENA AND THAT DIABLO GUY.
EXIT
WE NEED A FOOLPROOF PLAN FOR GETTING THEM.
WELL THEN YOU SHOULDN'T HAVE FOOLS COMING UP WITH THE PLAN. YOU SHOULD BE EMPLOYING THE BRILLIANCE AND SUPERIOR INTELLIGENCE OF--

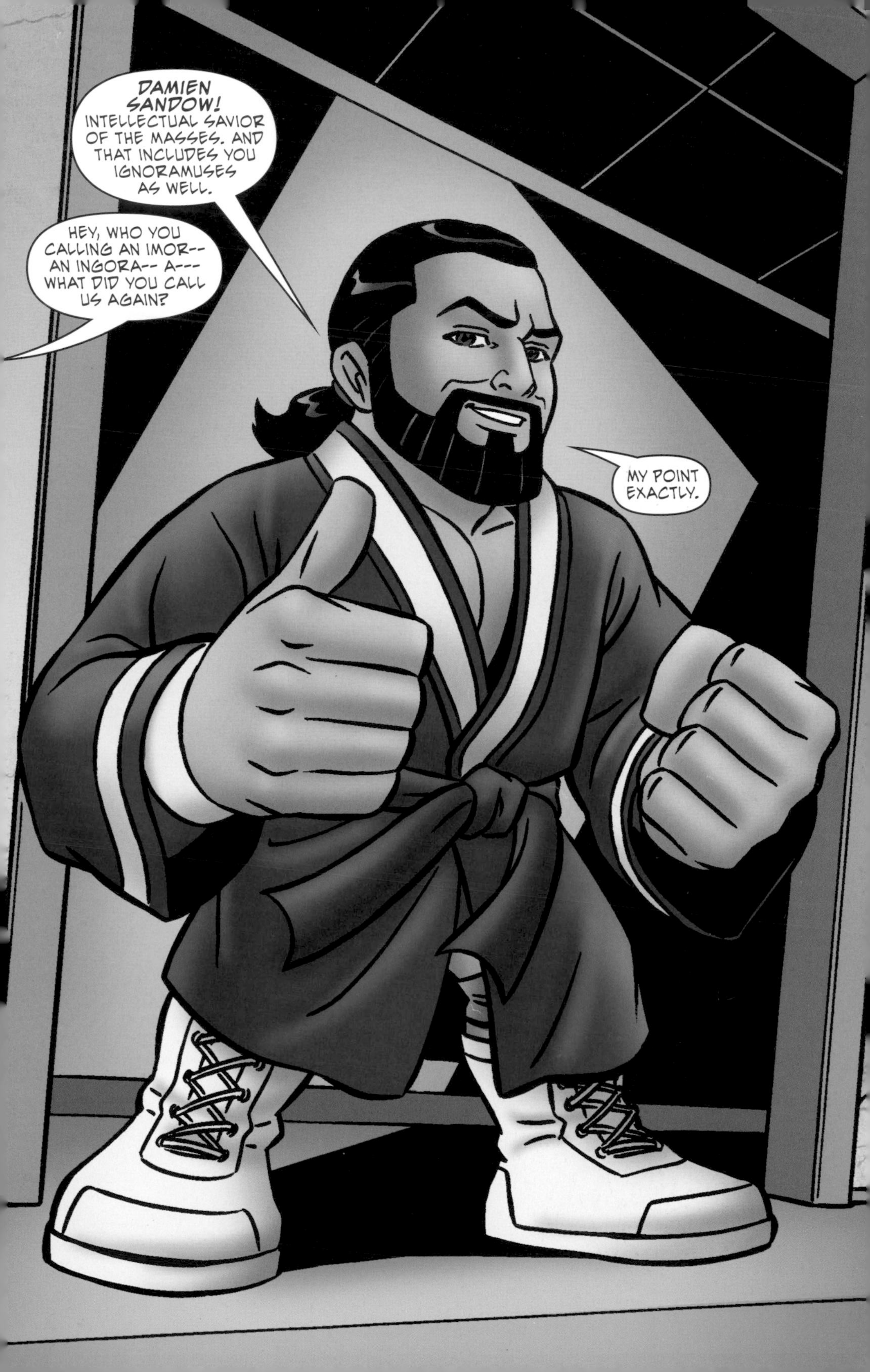
DAMIEN SANDOW! INTELLECTUAL SAVIOR OF THE MASSES. AND THAT INCLUDES YOU IGNORAMUSES AS WELL.
HEY, WHO YOU CALLING AN IMOR-- AN INGORA-- A--- WHAT DID YOU CALL US AGAIN?
MY POINT EXACTLY.

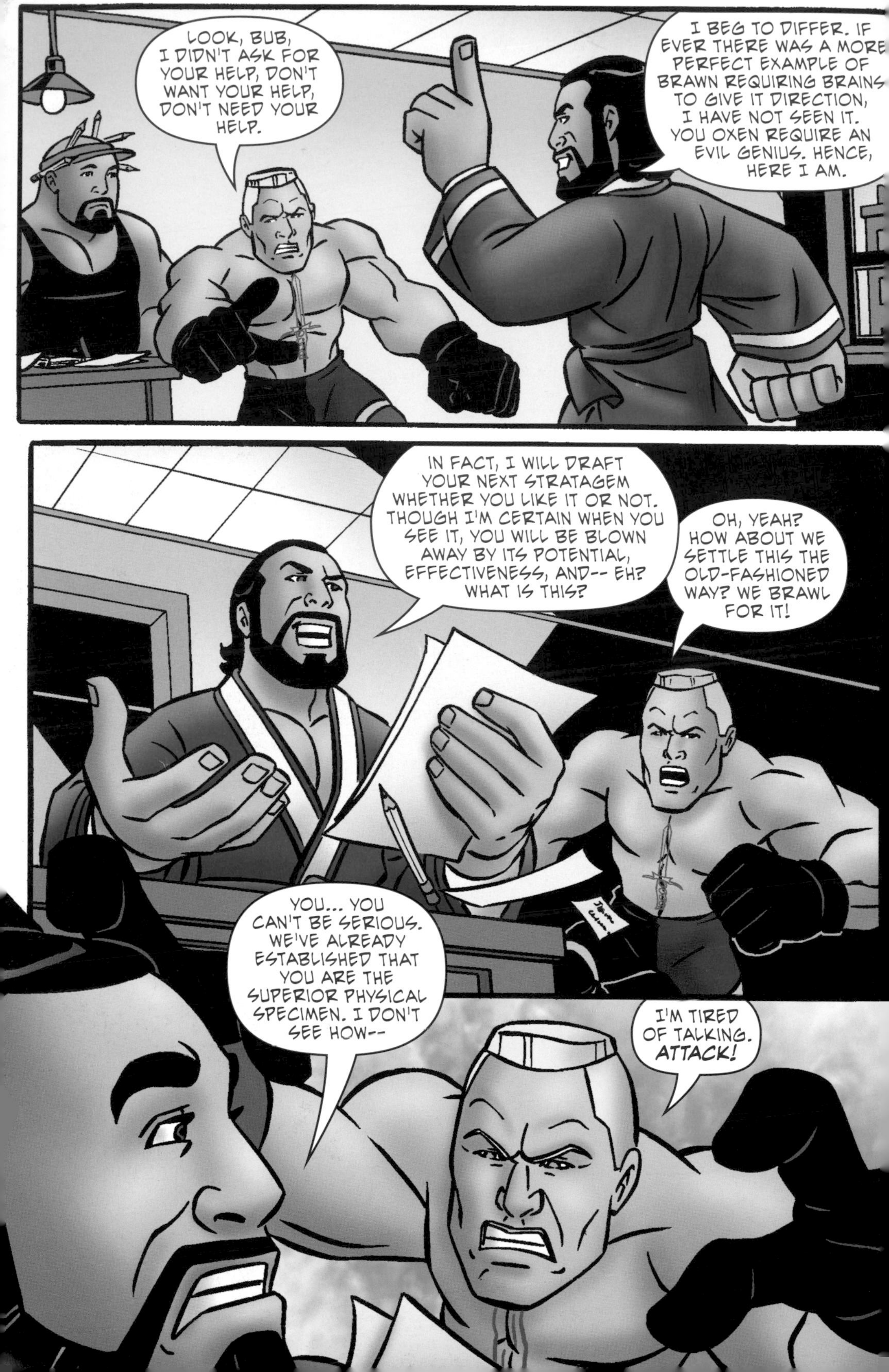
LOOK, BUB, I DIDN'T ASK FOR YOUR HELP, DON'T WANT YOUR HELP, DON'T NEED YOUR HELP.
I BEG TO DIFFER. IF EVER THERE WAS A MORE PERFECT EXAMPLE OF BRAWN REQUIRING BRAINS TO GIVE IT DIRECTION, I HAVE NOT SEEN IT. YOU OXEN REQUIRE AN EVIL GENIUS. HENCE, HERE I AM.
IN FACT, I WILL DRAFT YOUR NEXT STRATAGEM WHETHER YOU LIKE IT OR NOT. THOUGH I'M CERTAIN WHEN YOU SEE IT, YOU WILL BE BLOWN AWAY BY ITS POTENTIAL, EFFECTIVENESS, AND-- EH? WHAT IS THIS?
OH, YEAH? HOW ABOUT WE SETTLE THIS THE OLD-FASHIONED WAY? WE BRAWL FOR IT!
YOU... YOU CAN'T BE SERIOUS. WE'VE ALREADY ESTABLISHED THAT YOU ARE THE SUPERIOR PHYSICAL SPECIMEN. I DON'T SEE HOW--
I'M TIRED OF TALKING. ATTACK!

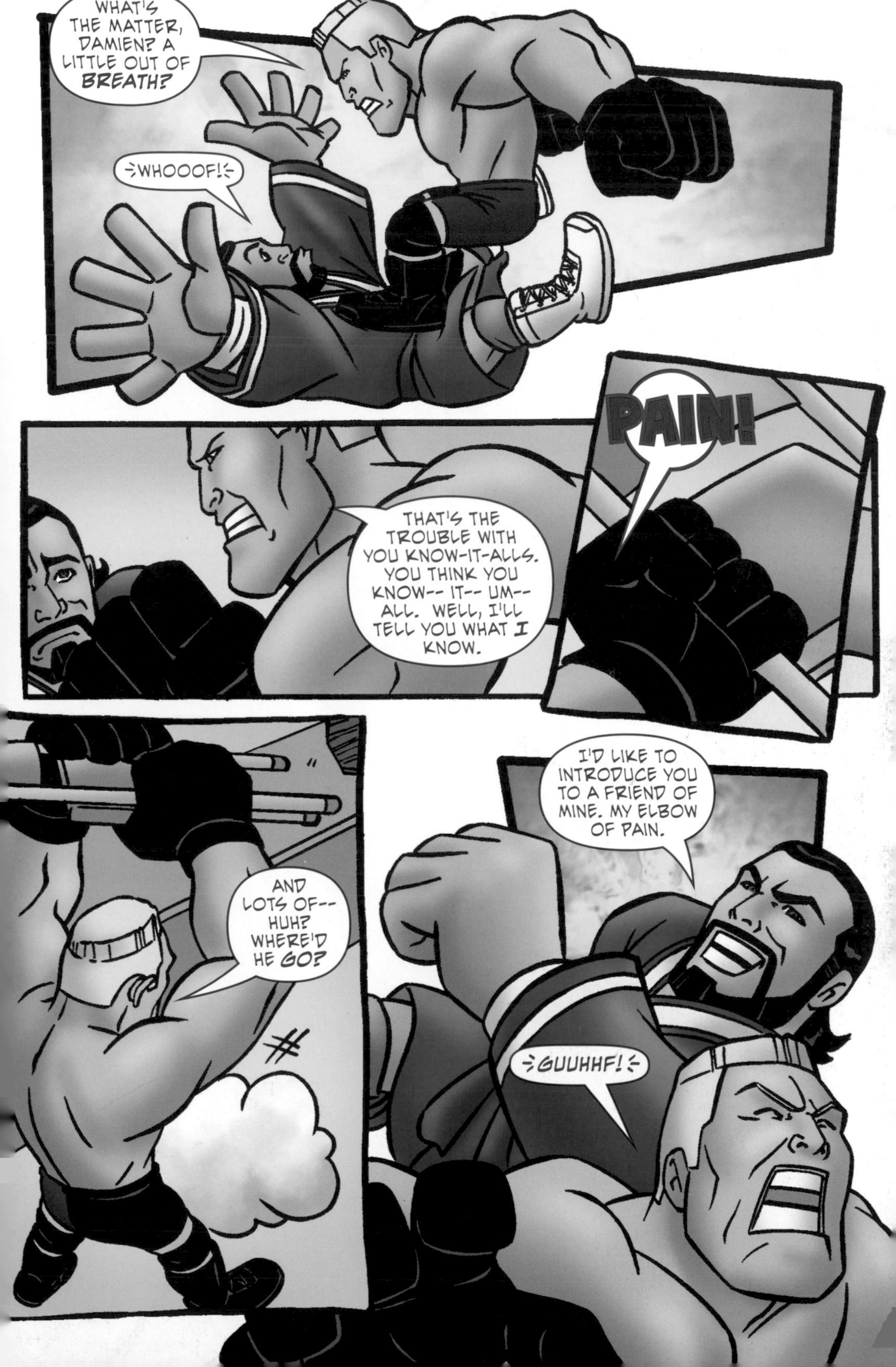
WHAT'S THE MATTER, DAMIEN? A LITTLE OUT OF BREATH?
WHOOOF!
PAIN!
THAT'S THE TROUBLE WITH YOU KNOW-IT-ALLS. YOU THINK YOU KNOW-- IT-- UM-- ALL. WELL, I'LL TELL YOU WHAT I KNOW.
AND LOTS OF-- HUH? WHERE'D HE GO?
I'D LIKE TO INTRODUCE YOU TO A FRIEND OF MINE. MY ELBOW OF PAIN.
GUUHHF!

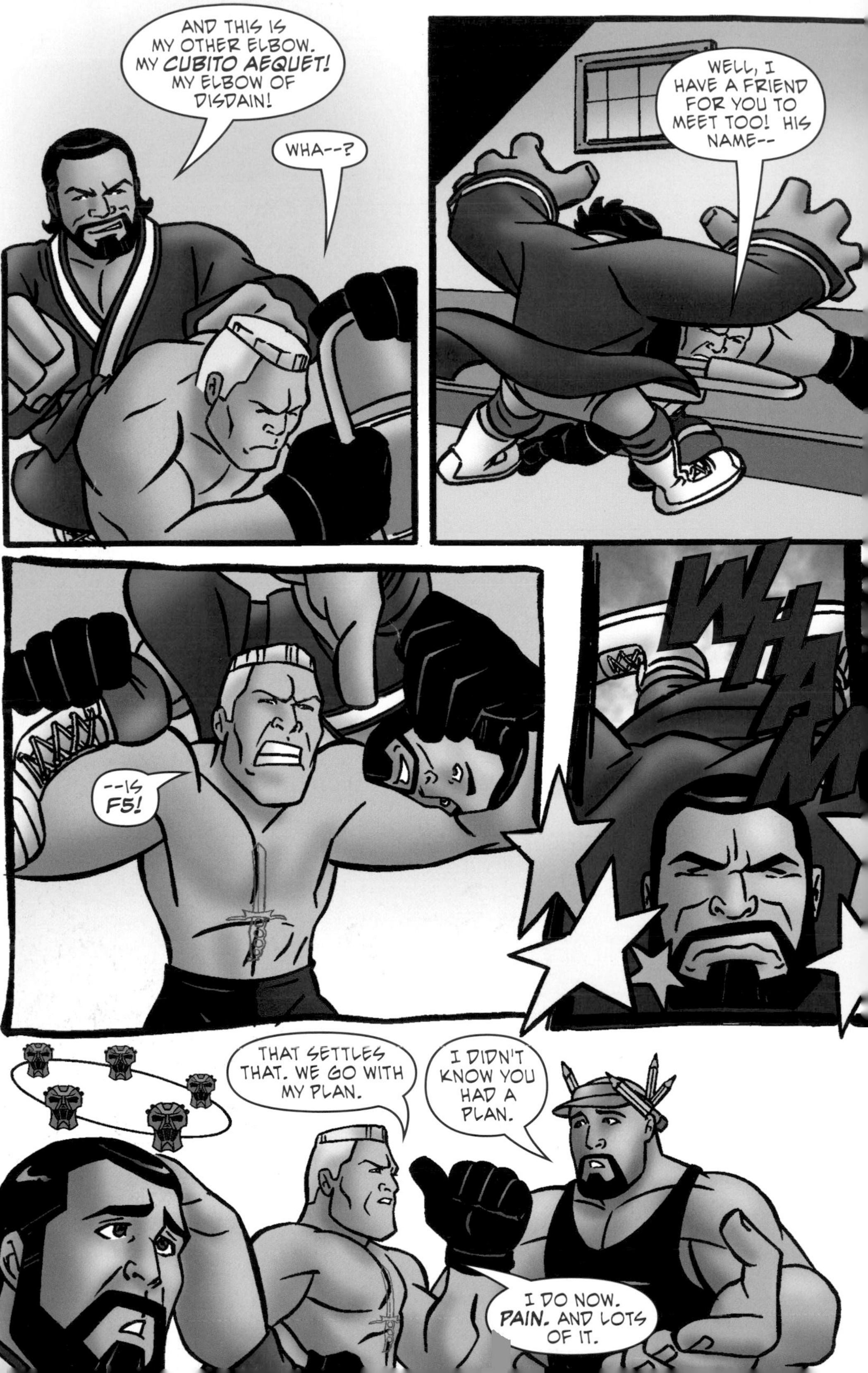
AND THIS IS MY OTHER ELBOW. MY CUBITO AEQUET! MY ELBOW OF DISDAIN!
WHA--?
WELL, I HAVE A FRIEND FOR YOU TO MEET TOO! HIS NAME--
--IS F5!
WHAM
THAT SETTLES THAT. WE GO WITH MY PLAN.
I DIDN'T KNOW YOU HAD A PLAN.
I DO NOW. PAIN. AND LOTS OF IT.

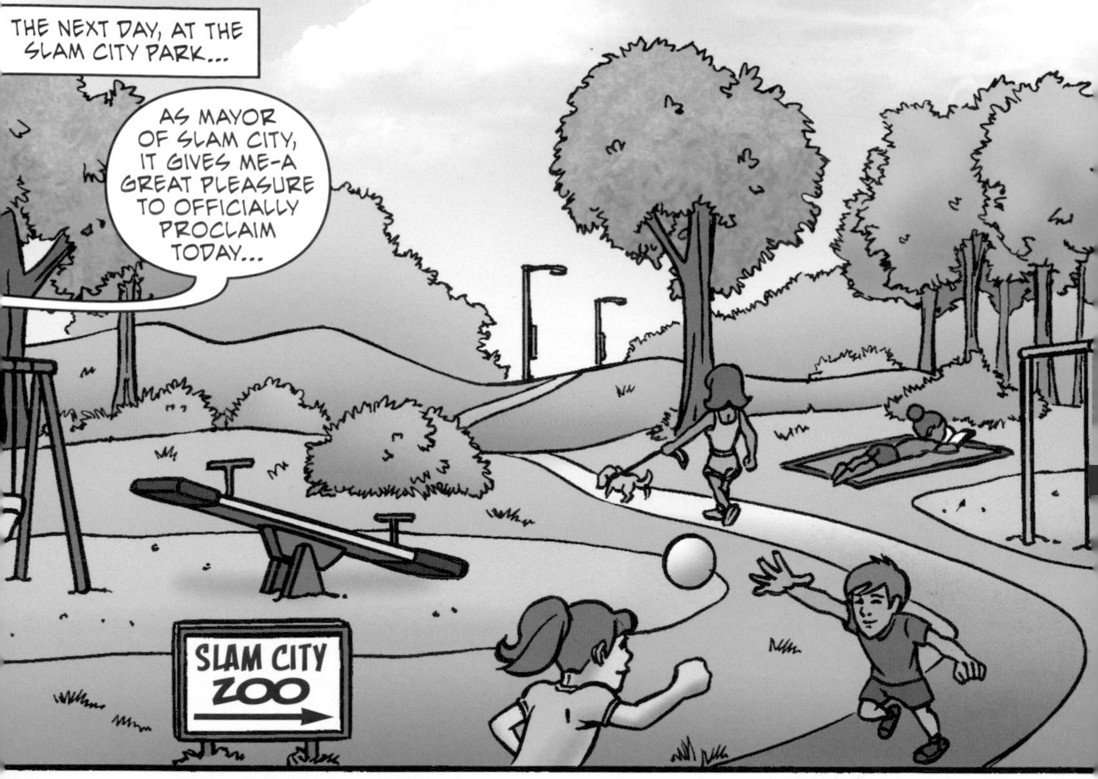
THE NEXT DAY, AT THE SLAM CITY PARK...
AS MAYOR OF SLAM CITY, IT GIVES ME-A GREAT PLEASURE TO OFFICIALLY PROCLAIM TODAY...
SLAM CITY ZOO

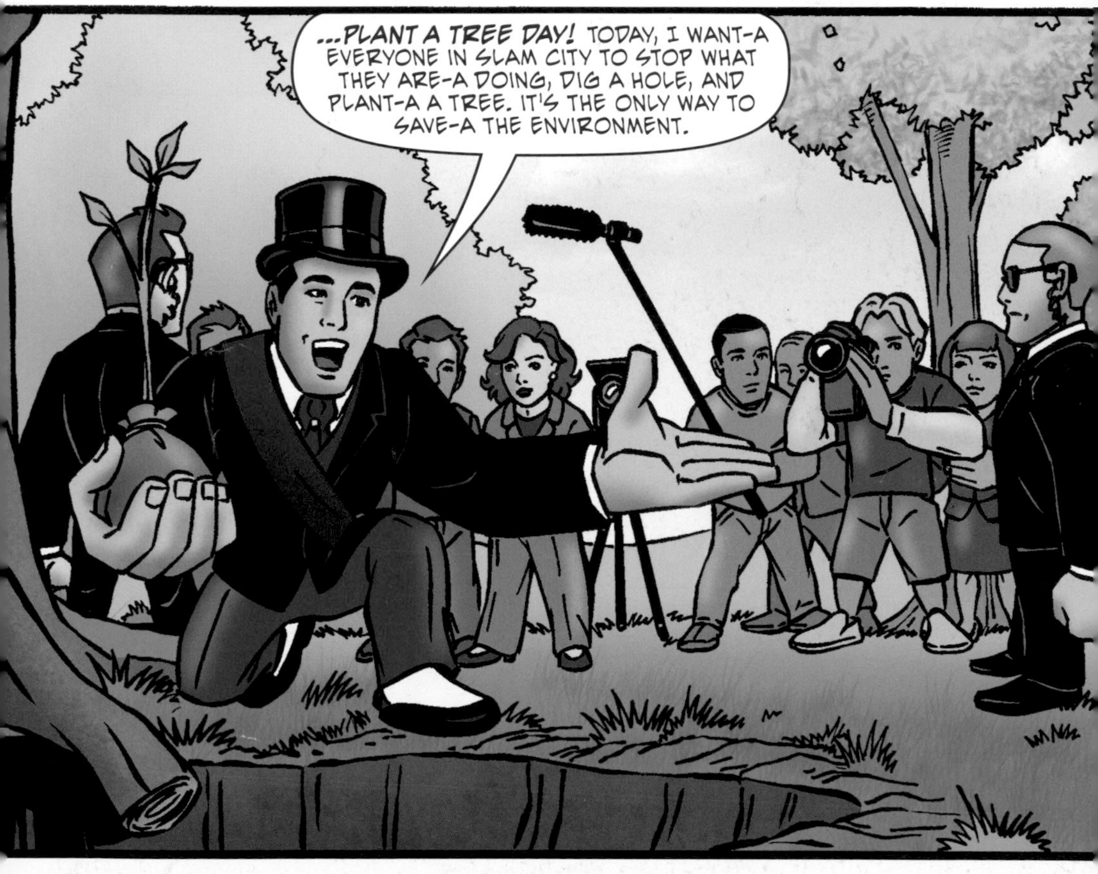
...PLANT A TREE DAY! TODAY, I WANT-A EVERYONE IN SLAM CITY TO STOP WHAT THEY ARE-A DOING, DIG A HOLE, AND PLANT-A A TREE. IT'S THE ONLY WAY TO SAVE-A THE ENVIRONMENT.

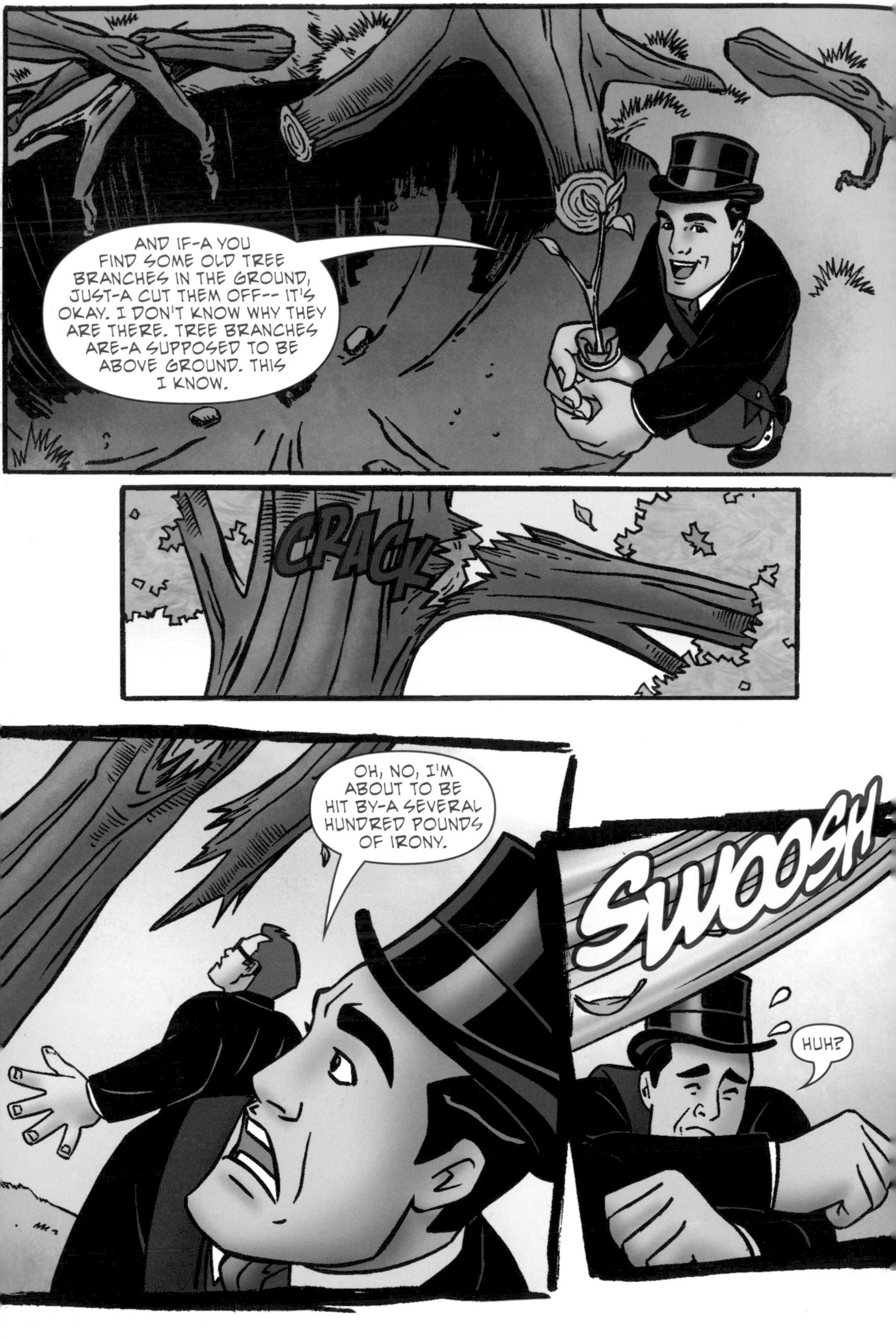
AND IF-A YOU FIND SOME OLD TREE BRANCHES IN THE GROUND, JUST-A CUT THEM OFF-- IT'S OKAY. I DON'T KNOW WHY THEY ARE THERE. TREE BRANCHES ARE-A SUPPOSED TO BE ABOVE GROUND. THIS I KNOW.
CRACK
OH, NO, I'M ABOUT TO BE HIT BY-A SEVERAL HUNDRED POUNDS OF IRONY.
SWOOSH
HUH?

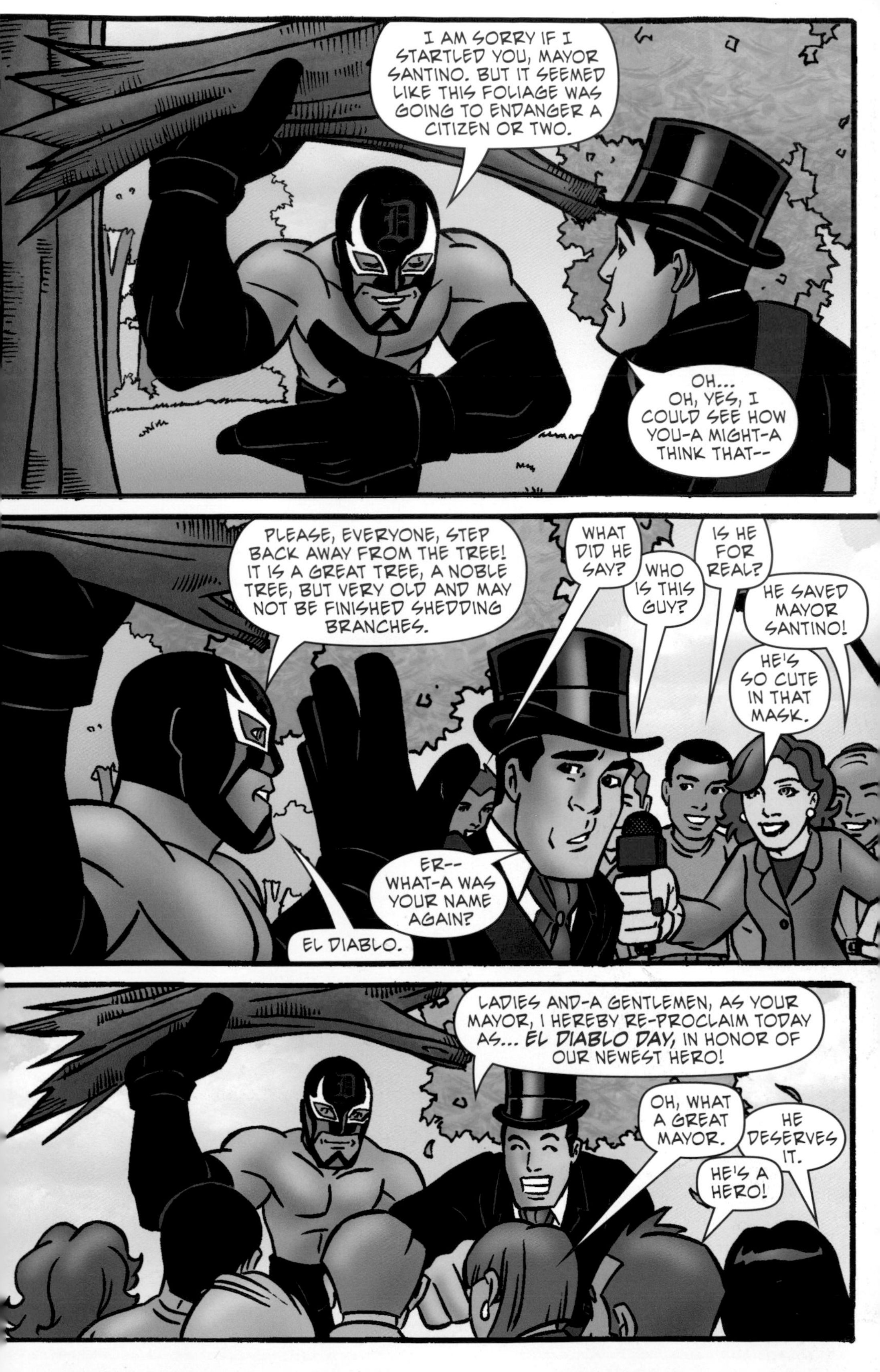
I AM SORRY IF I STARTLED YOU, MAYOR SANTINO. BUT IT SEEMED LIKE THIS FOLIAGE WAS GOING TO ENDANGER A CITIZEN OR TWO.
OH... OH, YES, I COULD SEE HOW YOU-A MIGHT-A THINK THAT--
PLEASE, EVERYONE, STEP BACK AWAY FROM THE TREE! IT IS A GREAT TREE, A NOBLE TREE, BUT VERY OLD AND MAY NOT BE FINISHED SHEDDING BRANCHES.
WHAT DID HE SAY?
WHO IS THIS GUY?
IS HE FOR REAL?
HE SAVED MAYOR SANTINO!
HE'S SO CUTE IN THAT MASK.
ER-- WHAT-A WAS YOUR NAME AGAIN?
EL DIABLO.
LADIES AND-A GENTLEMEN, AS YOUR MAYOR, I HEREBY RE-PROCLAIM TODAY AS... EL DIABLO DAY, IN HONOR OF OUR NEWEST HERO!
OH, WHAT A GREAT MAYOR.
HE DESERVES IT.
HE'S A HERO!

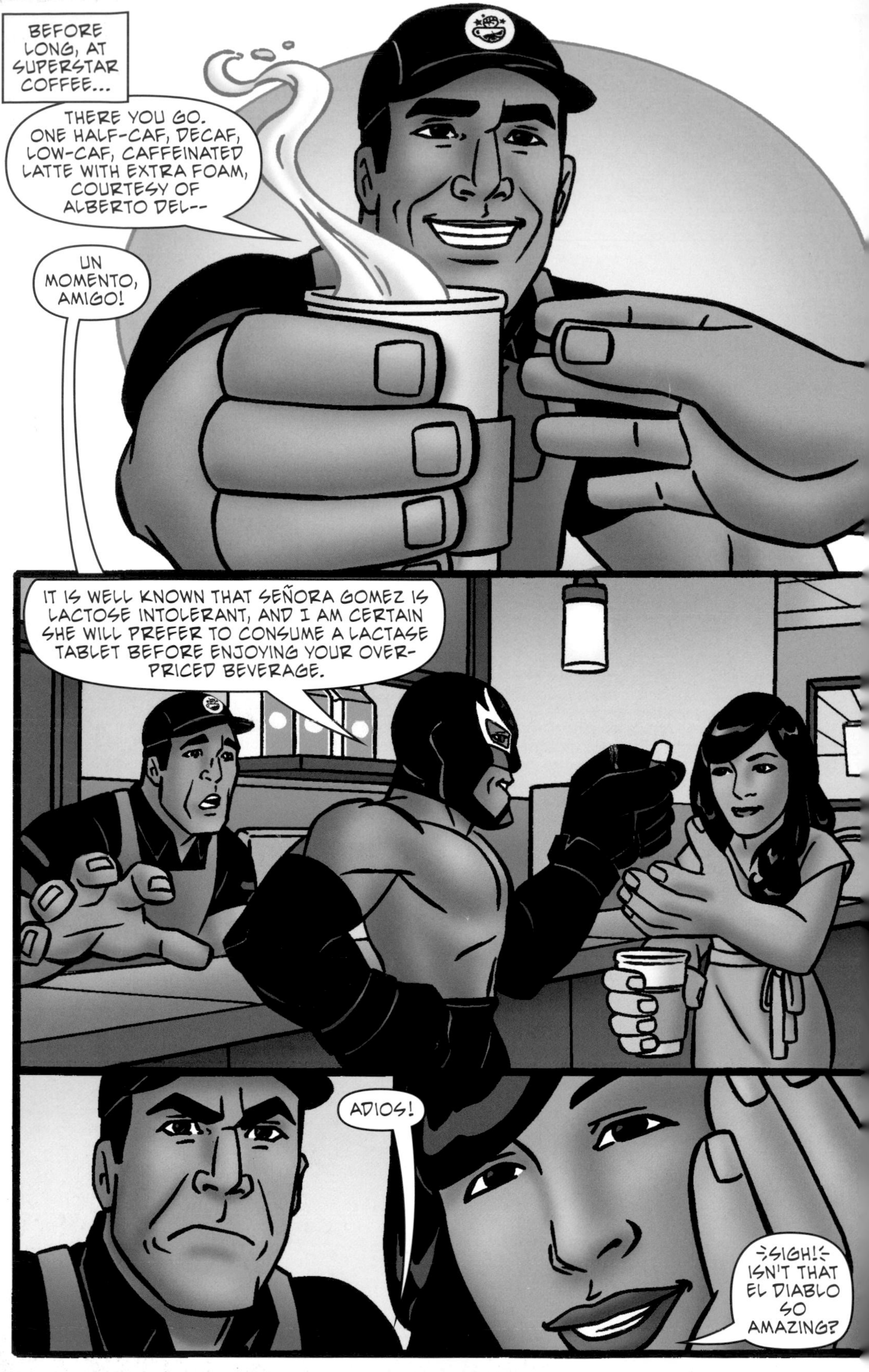
BEFORE LONG, AT SUPERSTAR COFFEE...
THERE YOU GO. ONE HALF-CAF, DECAF, LOW-CAF, CAFFEINATED LATTE WITH EXTRA FOAM, COURTESY OF ALBERTO DEL--
UN MOMENTO, AMIGO!
IT IS WELL KNOWN THAT SEÑORA GOMEZ IS LACTOSE INTOLERANT, AND I AM CERTAIN SHE WILL PREFER TO CONSUME A LACTASE TABLET BEFORE ENJOYING YOUR OVER-PRICED BEVERAGE.
ADIOS!
SIGH! ISN'T THAT EL DIABLO SO AMAZING?

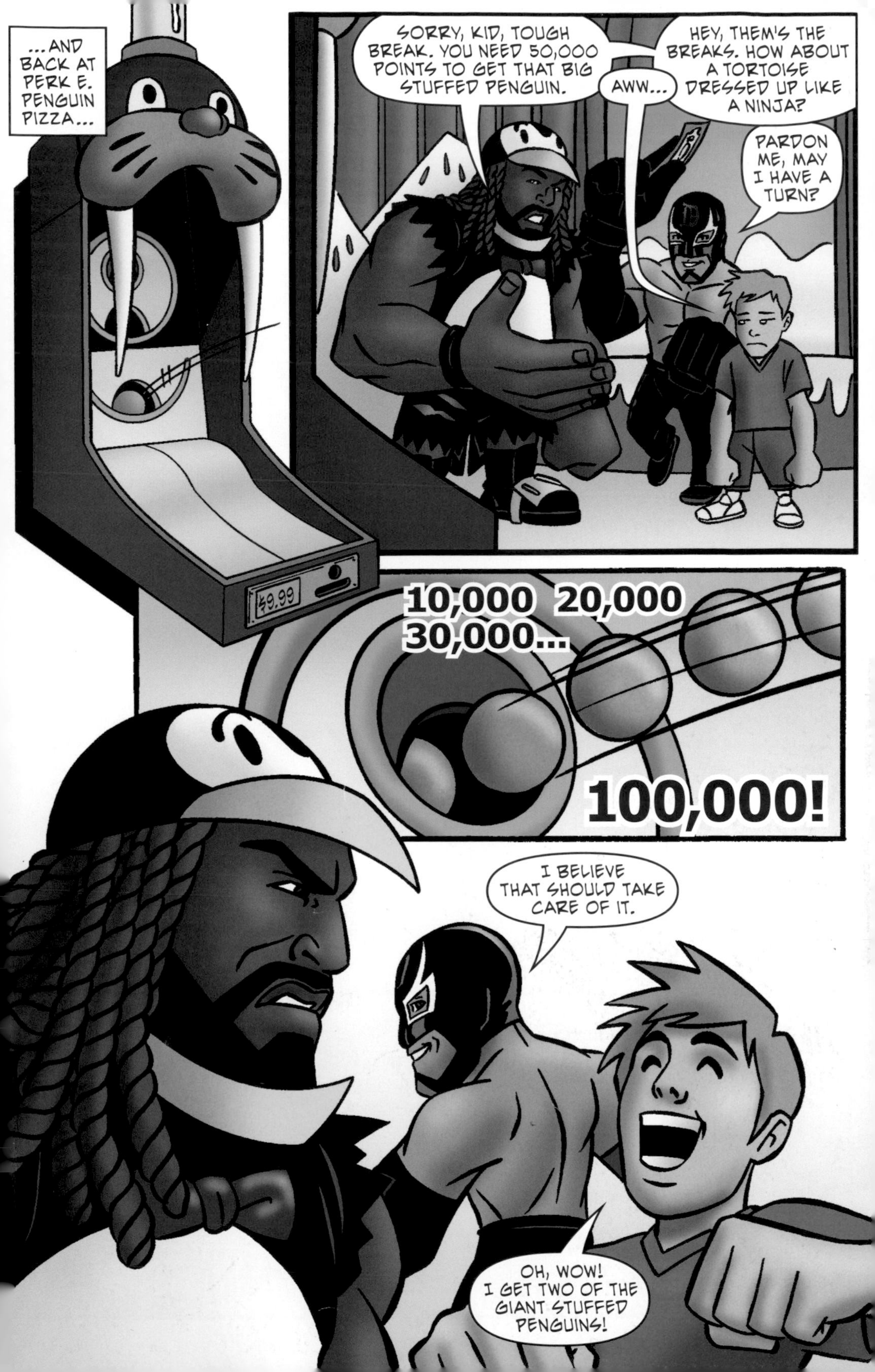
...AND BACK AT PERK E. PENGUIN PIZZA...
SORRY, KID, TOUGH BREAK. YOU NEED 50,000 POINTS TO GET THAT BIG STUFFED PENGUIN.
AWW...
HEY, THEM'S THE BREAKS. HOW ABOUT A TORTOISE DRESSED UP LIKE A NINJA?
PARDON ME, MAY I HAVE A TURN?
$9.99
10,000 20,000 30,000...
100,000!
I BELIEVE THAT SHOULD TAKE CARE OF IT.
OH, WOW! I GET TWO OF THE GIANT STUFFED PENGUINS!

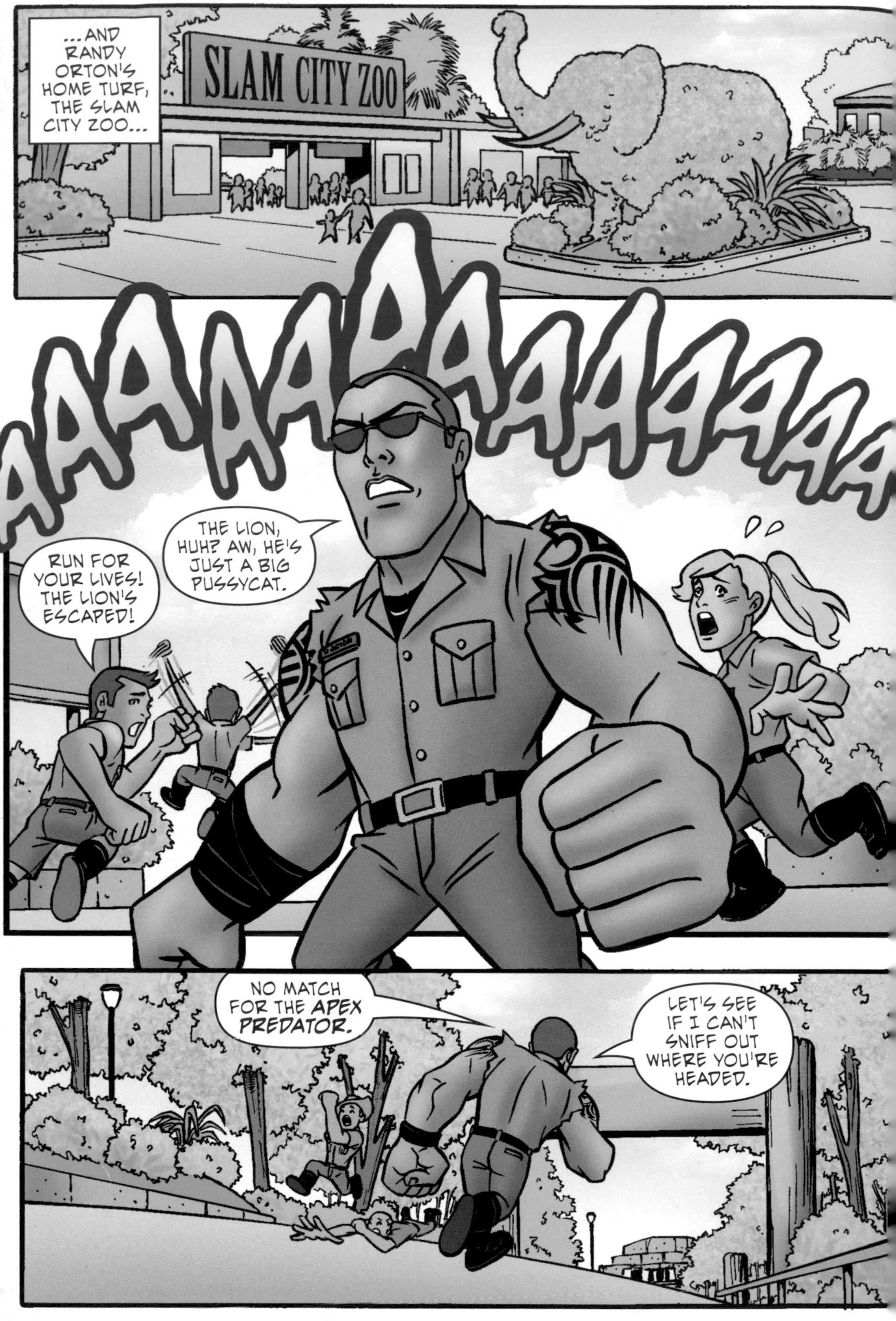
...AND RANDY ORTON'S HOME TURF, THE SLAM CITY ZOO...
SLAM CITY ZOO
AAAAAAAAAAAAAAA
RUN FOR YOUR LIVES! THE LION'S ESCAPED!
THE LION, HUH? AW, HE'S JUST A BIG PUSSYCAT.
NO MATCH FOR THE **APEX PREDATOR.**
LET'S SEE IF I CAN'T SNIFF OUT WHERE YOU'RE HEADED.

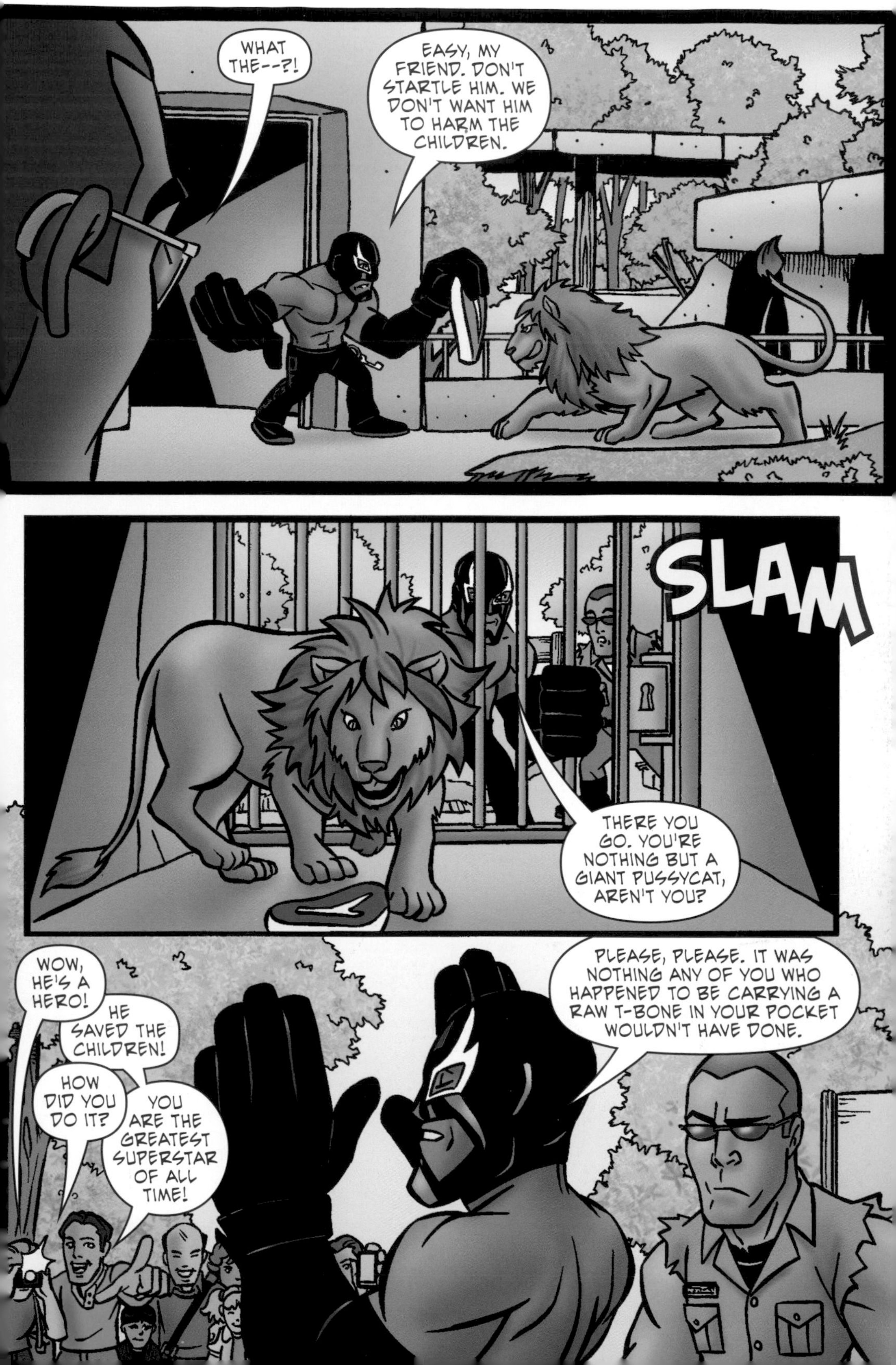
WHAT THE--?!
EASY, MY FRIEND. DON'T STARTLE HIM. WE DON'T WANT HIM TO HARM THE CHILDREN.
SLAM
THERE YOU GO. YOU'RE NOTHING BUT A GIANT PUSSYCAT, AREN'T YOU?
WOW, HE'S A HERO!
HE SAVED THE CHILDREN!
HOW DID YOU DO IT?
YOU ARE THE GREATEST SUPERSTAR OF ALL TIME!
PLEASE, PLEASE. IT WAS NOTHING ANY OF YOU WHO HAPPENED TO BE CARRYING A RAW T-BONE IN YOUR POCKET WOULDN'T HAVE DONE.

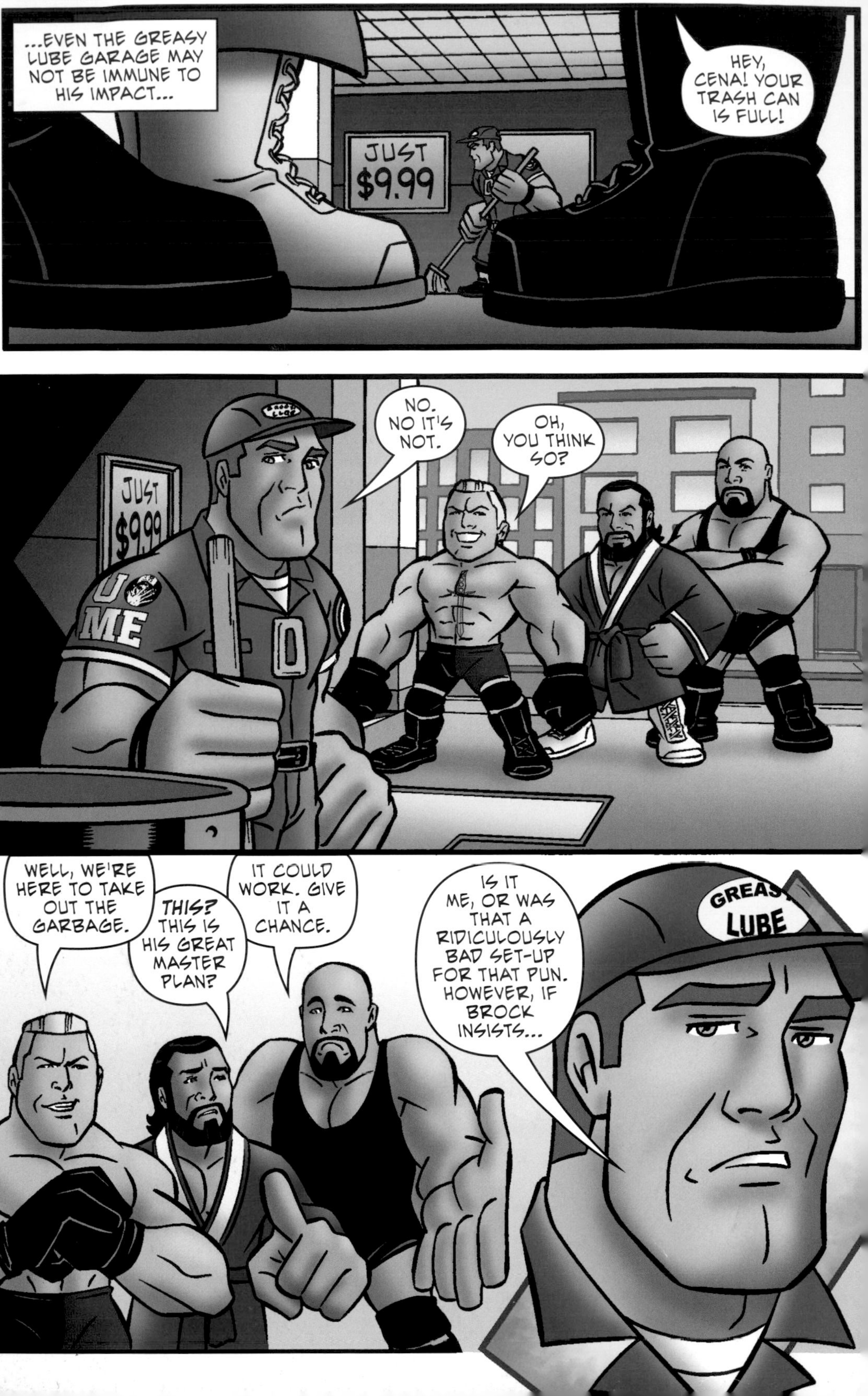
...EVEN THE GREASY LUBE GARAGE MAY NOT BE IMMUNE TO HIS IMPACT...
HEY, CENA! YOUR TRASH CAN IS FULL!
JUST $9.99
NO. NO IT'S NOT.
OH, YOU THINK SO?
U ME
WELL, WE'RE HERE TO TAKE OUT THE GARBAGE.
THIS? THIS IS HIS GREAT MASTER PLAN?
IT COULD WORK. GIVE IT A CHANCE.
IS IT ME, OR WAS THAT A RIDICULOUSLY BAD SET-UP FOR THAT PUN. HOWEVER, IF BROCK INSISTS...
LUBE

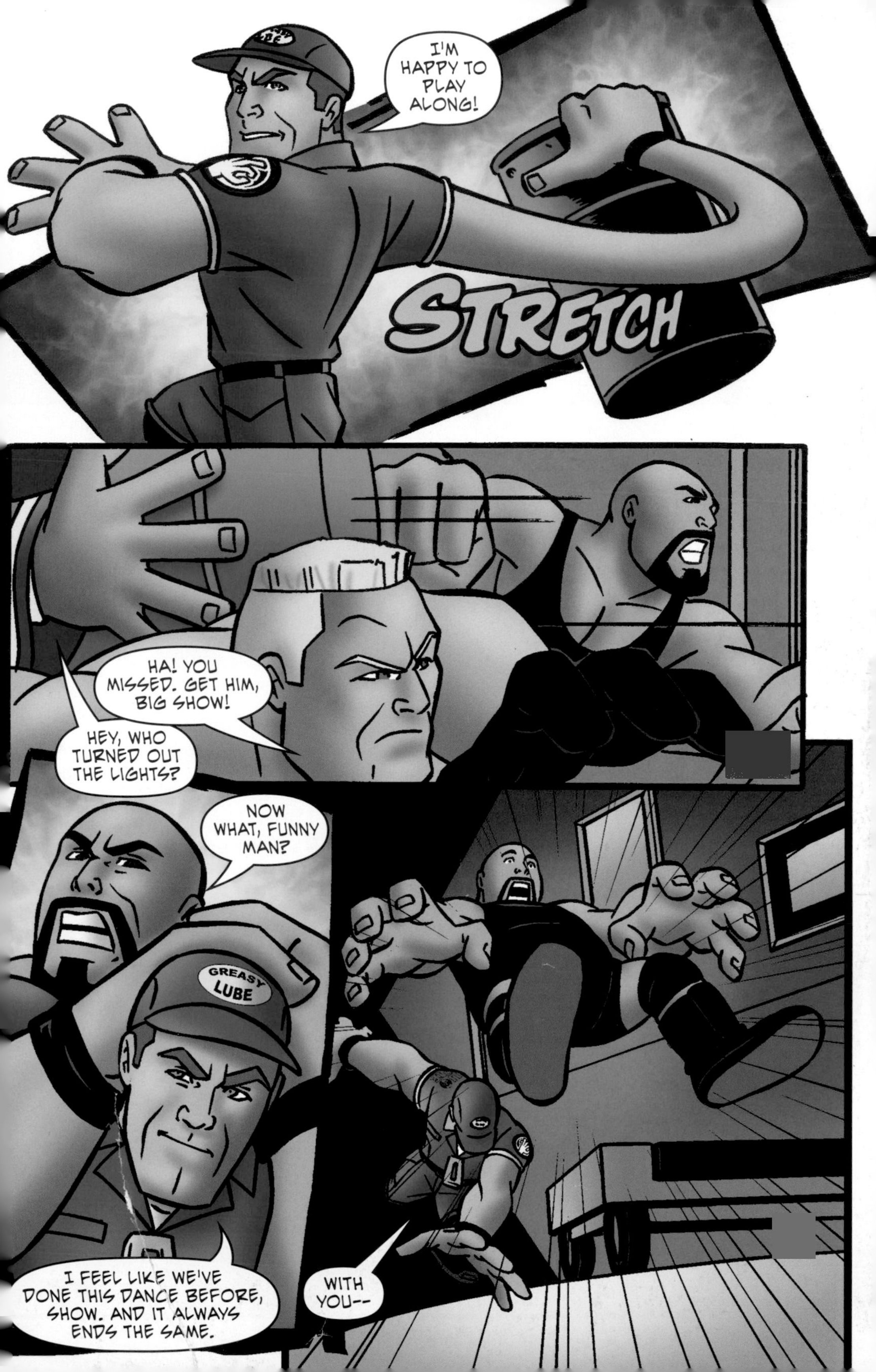
I'M HAPPY TO PLAY ALONG!
STRETCH
HA! YOU MISSED. GET HIM, BIG SHOW!
HEY, WHO TURNED OUT THE LIGHTS?
NOW WHAT, FUNNY MAN?
GREASY LUBE
I FEEL LIKE WE'VE DONE THIS DANCE BEFORE, SHOW. AND IT ALWAYS ENDS THE SAME.
WITH YOU--

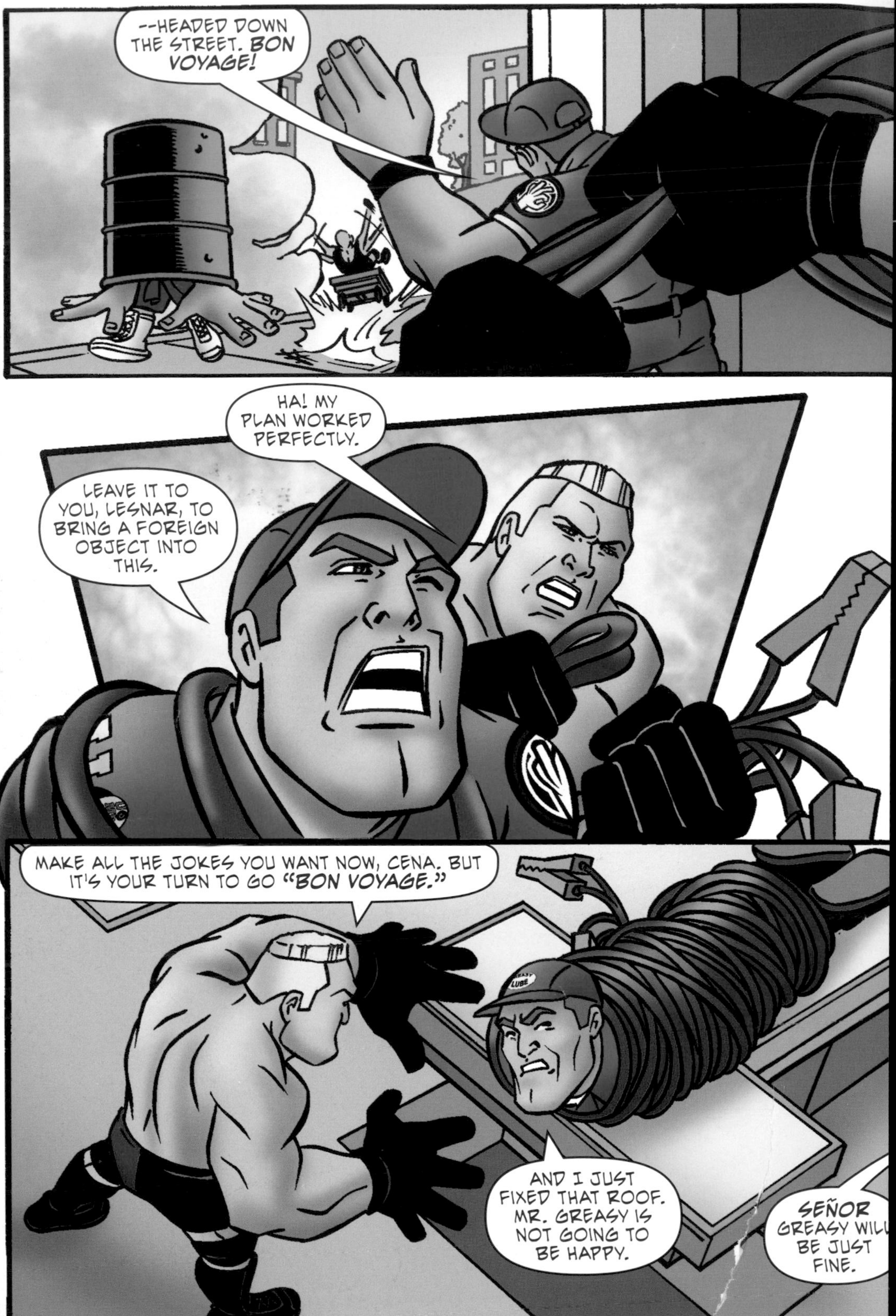
--HEADED DOWN THE STREET. BON VOYAGE!
HA! MY PLAN WORKED PERFECTLY.
LEAVE IT TO YOU, LESNAR, TO BRING A FOREIGN OBJECT INTO THIS.
MAKE ALL THE JOKES YOU WANT NOW, CENA. BUT IT'S YOUR TURN TO GO "BON VOYAGE."
AND I JUST FIXED THAT ROOF. MR. GREASY IS NOT GOING TO BE HAPPY.
SEÑOR GREASY WILL BE JUST FINE.

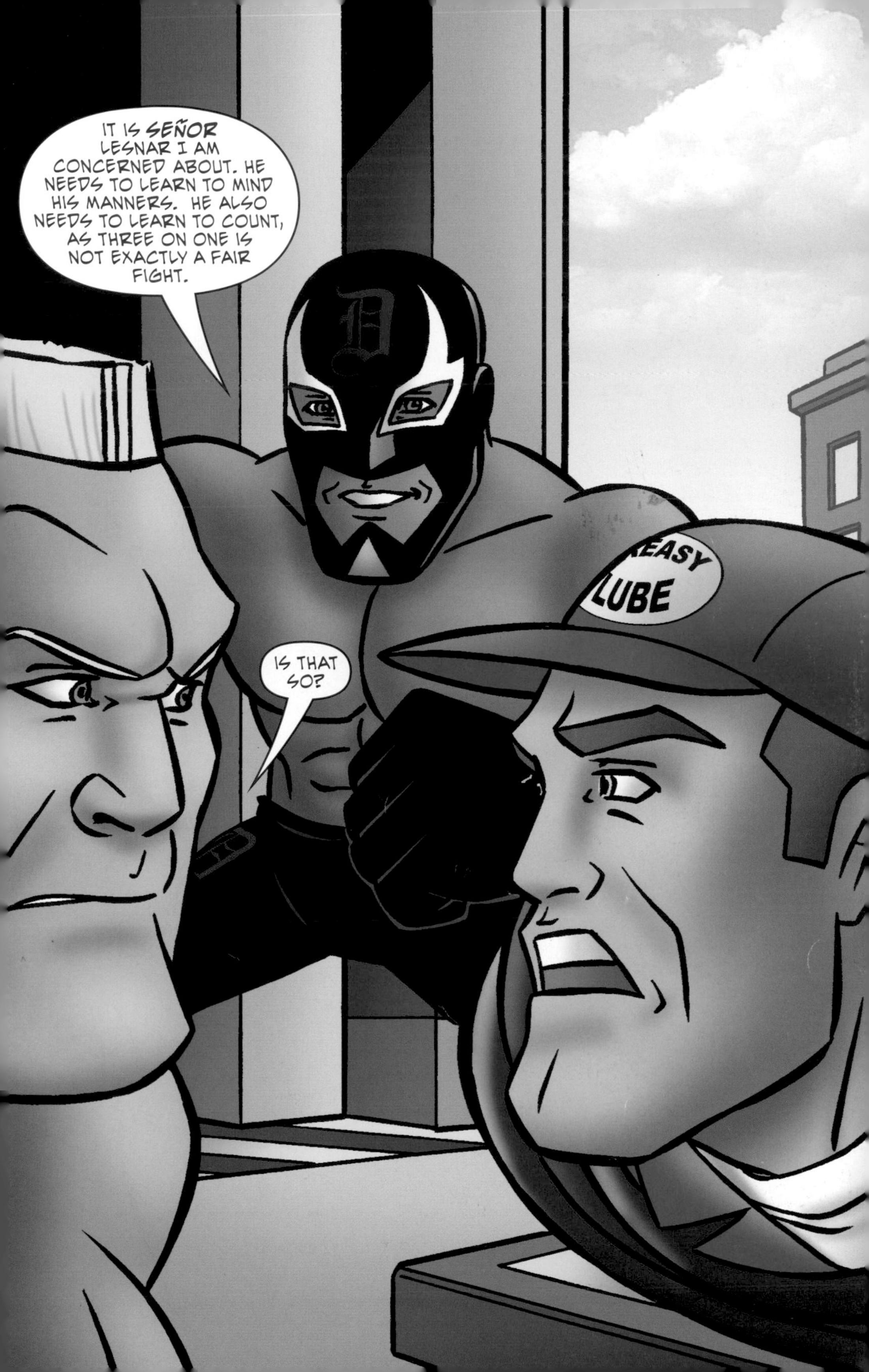
IT IS SEÑOR LESNAR I AM CONCERNED ABOUT. HE NEEDS TO LEARN TO MIND HIS MANNERS. HE ALSO NEEDS TO LEARN TO COUNT, AS THREE ON ONE IS NOT EXACTLY A FAIR FIGHT.
IS THAT SO?
LUBE

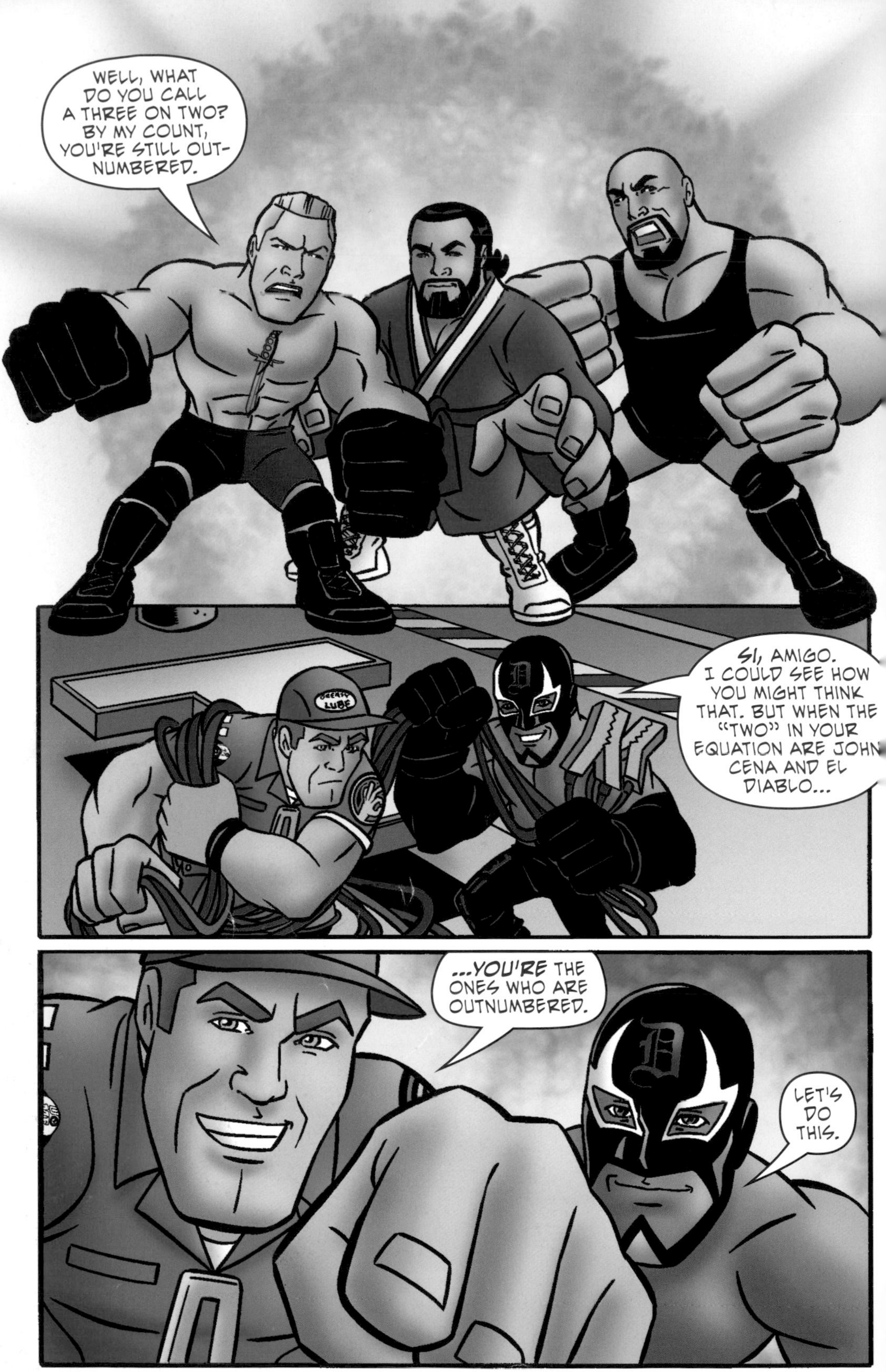
WELL, WHAT DO YOU CALL A THREE ON TWO? BY MY COUNT, YOU'RE STILL OUT-NUMBERED.
SI, AMIGO. I COULD SEE HOW YOU MIGHT THINK THAT. BUT WHEN THE "TWO" IN YOUR EQUATION ARE JOHN CENA AND EL DIABLO...
...YOU'RE THE ONES WHO ARE OUTNUMBERED.
LET'S DO THIS.

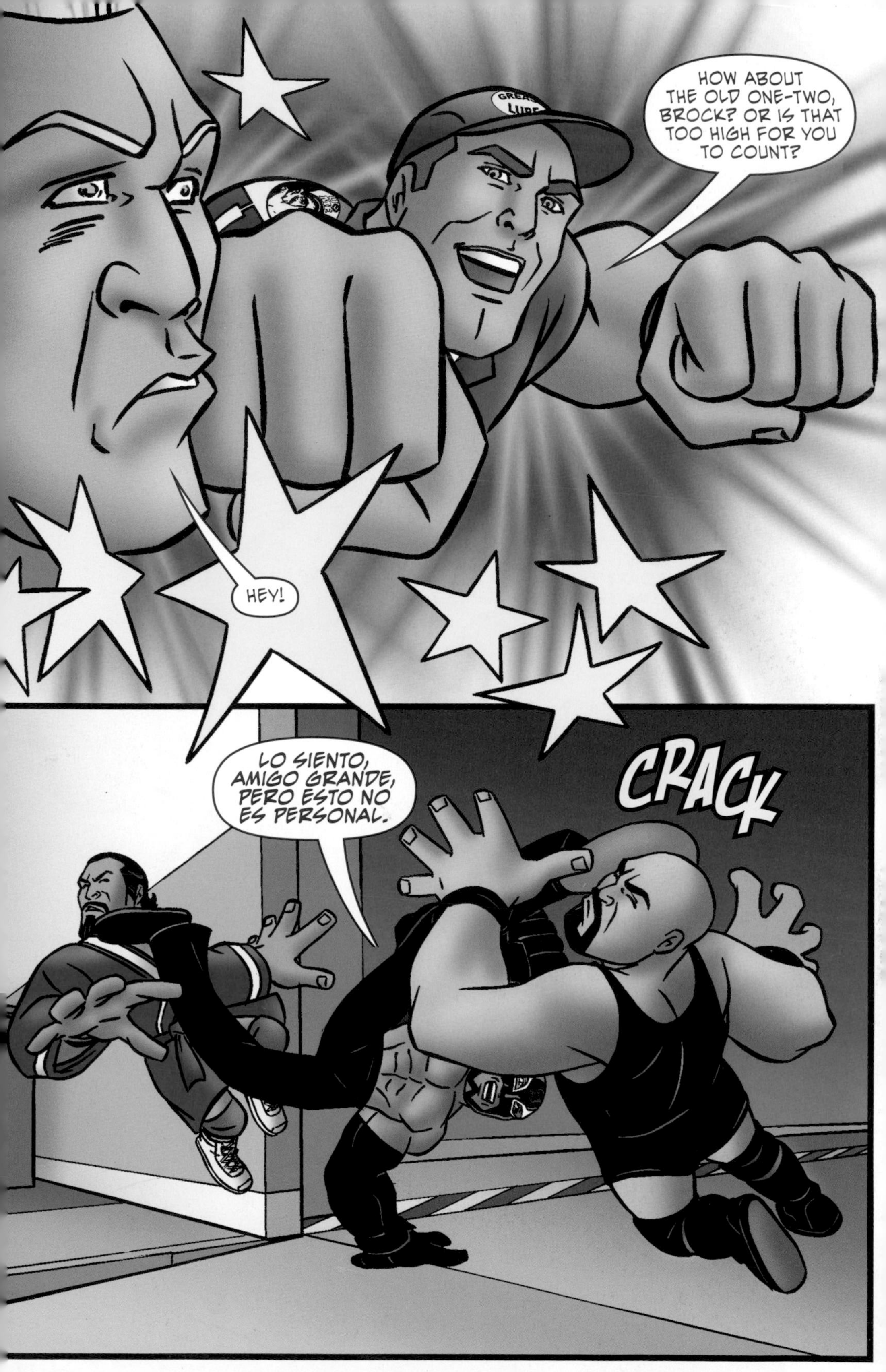
HOW ABOUT THE OLD ONE-TWO, BROCK? OR IS THAT TOO HIGH FOR YOU TO COUNT?
HEY!
LO SIENTO, AMIGO GRANDE, PERO ESTO NO ES PERSONAL.
CRACK

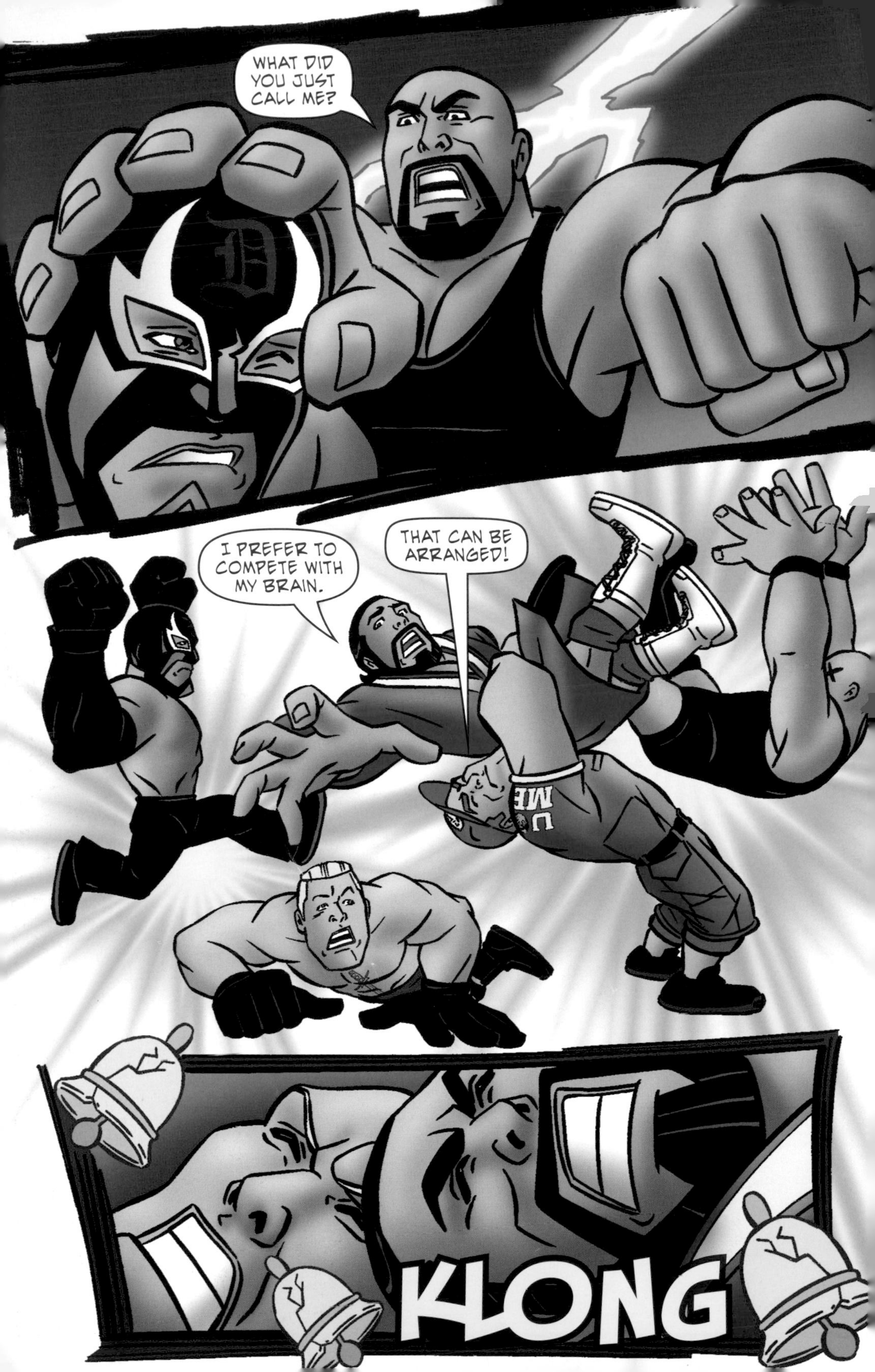
WHAT DID YOU JUST CALL ME?
I PREFER TO COMPETE WITH MY BRAIN.
THAT CAN BE ARRANGED!
KLONG

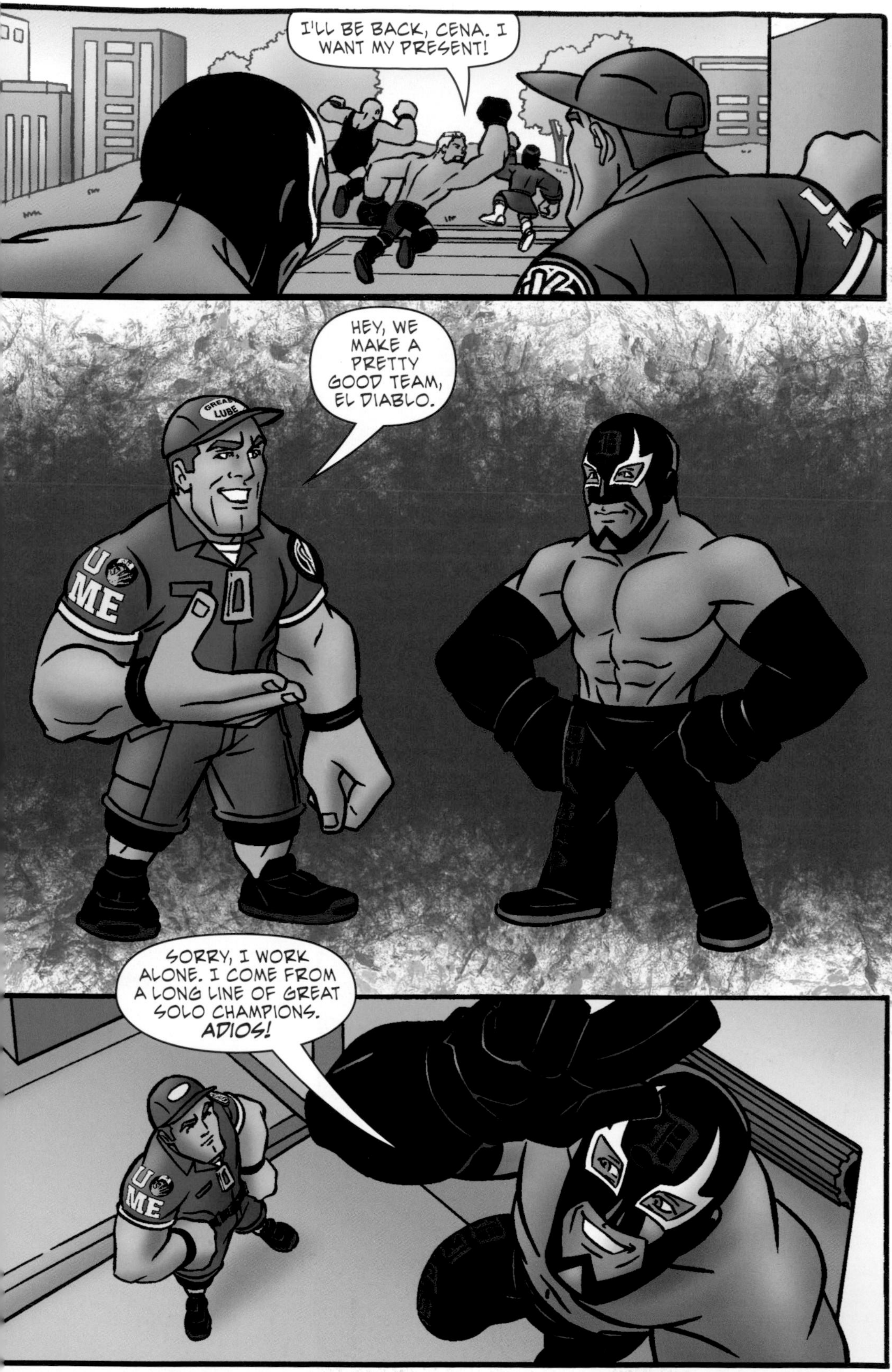
I'LL BE BACK, CENA. I WANT MY PRESENT!
HEY, WE MAKE A PRETTY GOOD TEAM, EL DIABLO.
GREAT LUBE
U C ME
SORRY, I WORK ALONE. I COME FROM A LONG LINE OF GREAT SOLO CHAMPIONS. ADIOS!

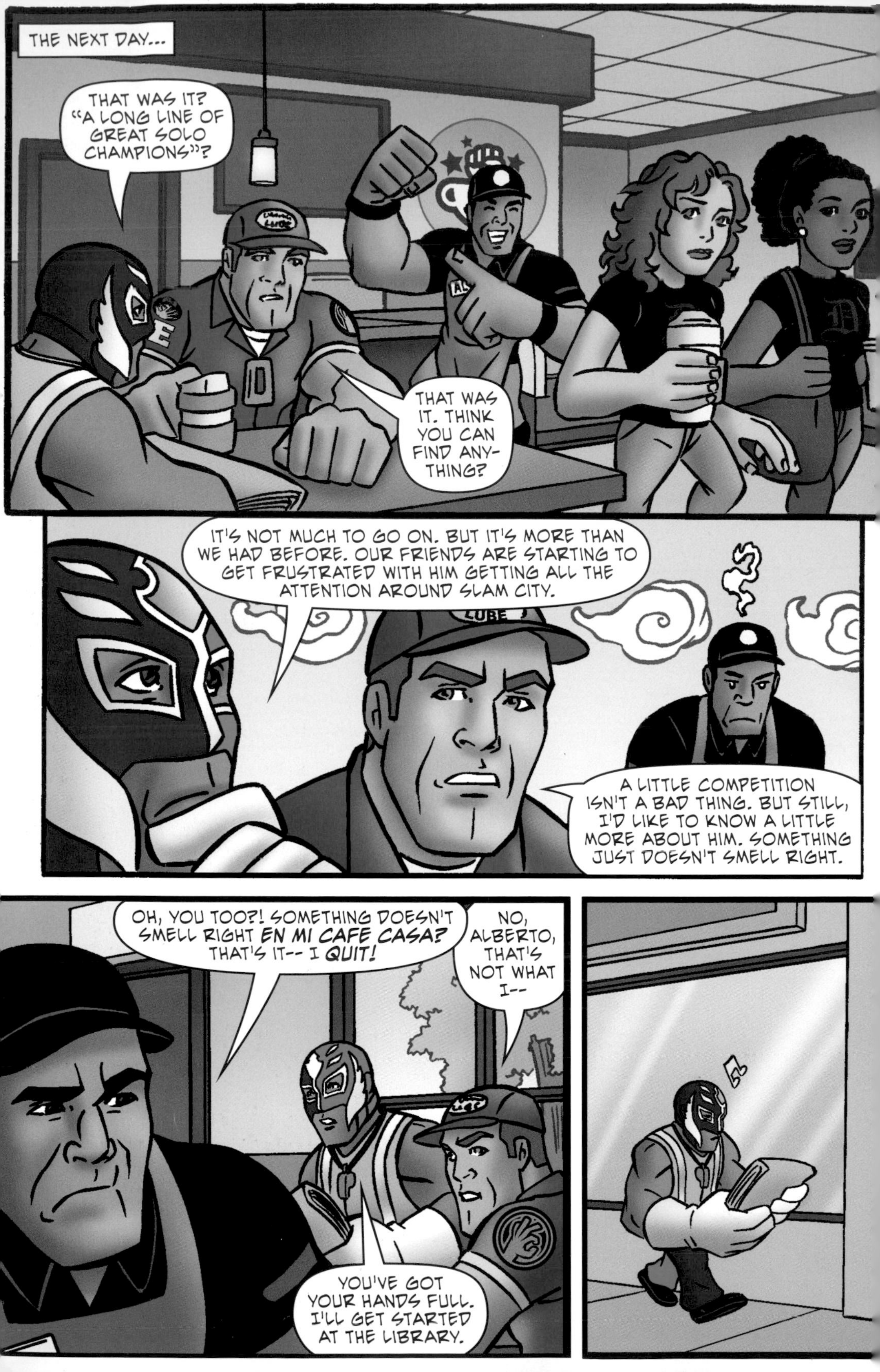
THE NEXT DAY...
THAT WAS IT? "A LONG LINE OF GREAT SOLO CHAMPIONS"?
THAT WAS IT. THINK YOU CAN FIND ANY-THING?
IT'S NOT MUCH TO GO ON. BUT IT'S MORE THAN WE HAD BEFORE. OUR FRIENDS ARE STARTING TO GET FRUSTRATED WITH HIM GETTING ALL THE ATTENTION AROUND SLAM CITY.
A LITTLE COMPETITION ISN'T A BAD THING. BUT STILL, I'D LIKE TO KNOW A LITTLE MORE ABOUT HIM. SOMETHING JUST DOESN'T SMELL RIGHT.
OH, YOU TOO?! SOMETHING DOESN'T SMELL RIGHT **EN MI CAFE CASA?** THAT'S IT-- I **QUIT!**
NO, ALBERTO, THAT'S NOT WHAT I--
YOU'VE GOT YOUR HANDS FULL. I'LL GET STARTED AT THE LIBRARY.

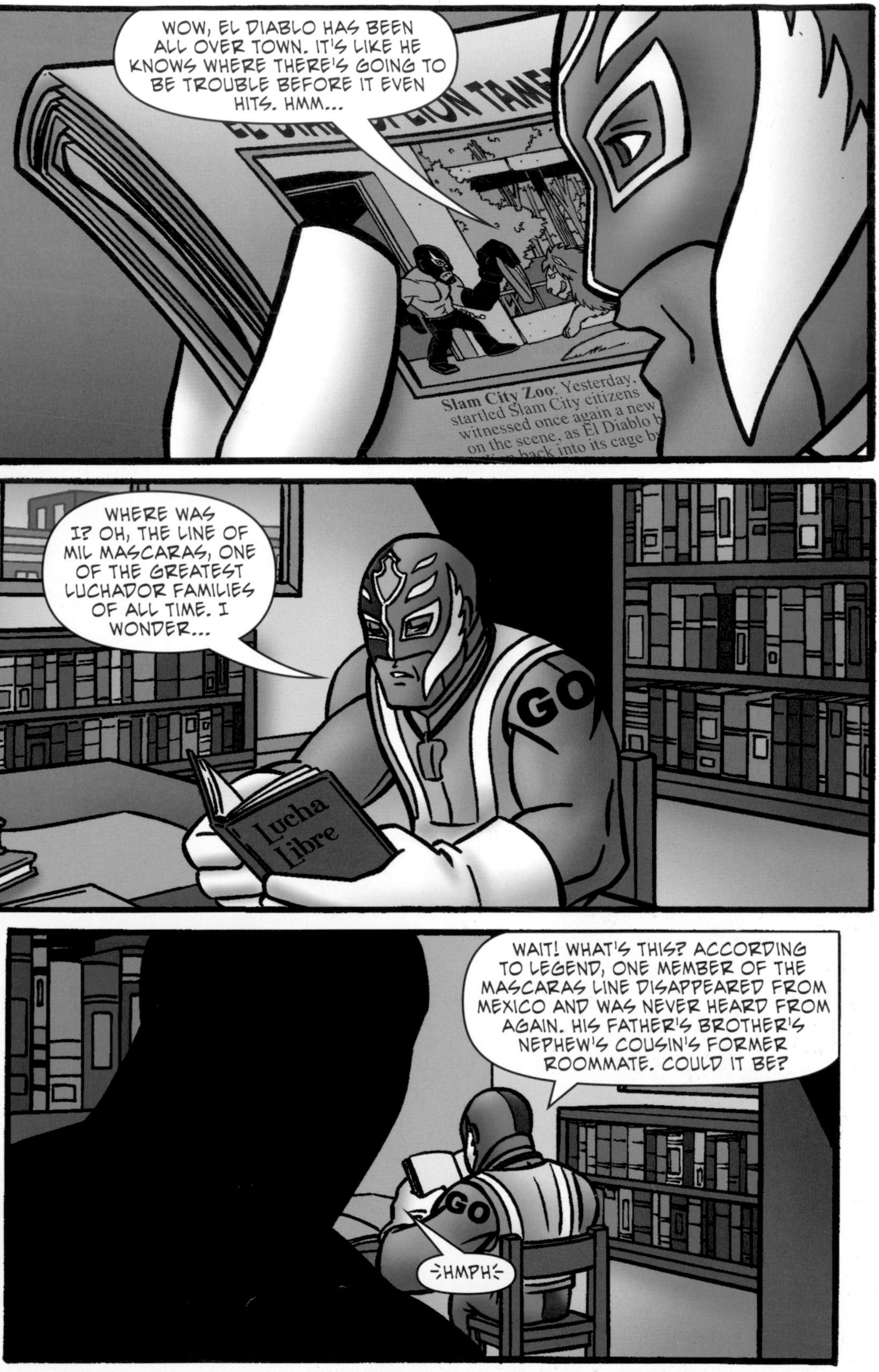
WOW, EL DIABLO HAS BEEN ALL OVER TOWN. IT'S LIKE HE KNOWS WHERE THERE'S GOING TO BE TROUBLE BEFORE IT EVEN HITS. HMM...
Slam City Zoo: Yesterday, startled Slam City citizens witnessed once again a new on the scene, as El Diablo b back into its cage b
WHERE WAS I? OH, THE LINE OF MIL MASCARAS, ONE OF THE GREATEST LUCHADOR FAMILIES OF ALL TIME. I WONDER...
Lucha Libre
GO
WAIT! WHAT'S THIS? ACCORDING TO LEGEND, ONE MEMBER OF THE MASCARAS LINE DISAPPEARED FROM MEXICO AND WAS NEVER HEARD FROM AGAIN. HIS FATHER'S BROTHER'S NEPHEW'S COUSIN'S FORMER ROOMMATE. COULD IT BE?
GO
HMPH

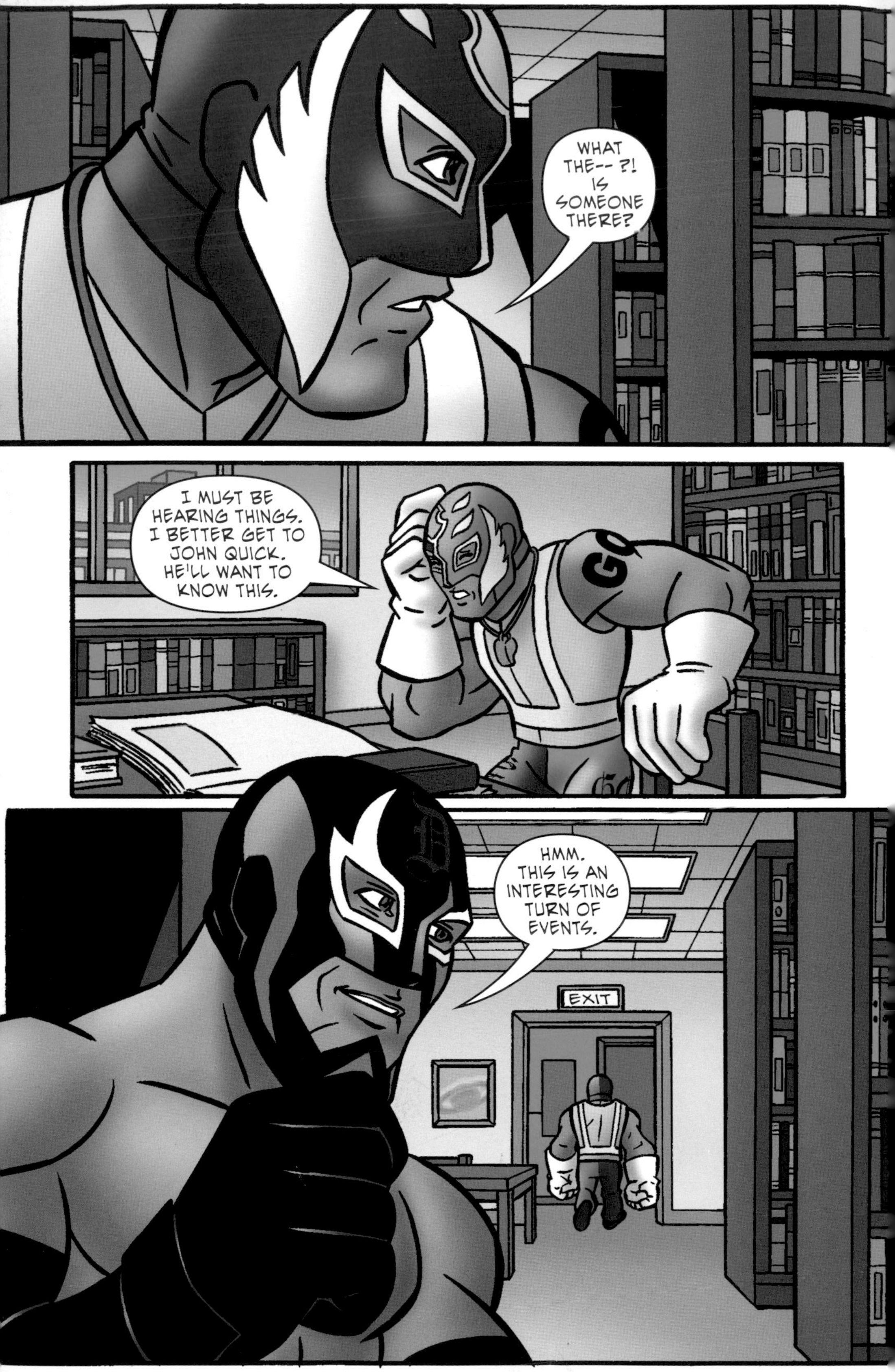
WHAT THE-- ?! IS SOMEONE THERE?
I MUST BE HEARING THINGS. I BETTER GET TO JOHN QUICK. HE'LL WANT TO KNOW THIS.
HMM. THIS IS AN INTERESTING TURN OF EVENTS.
EXIT

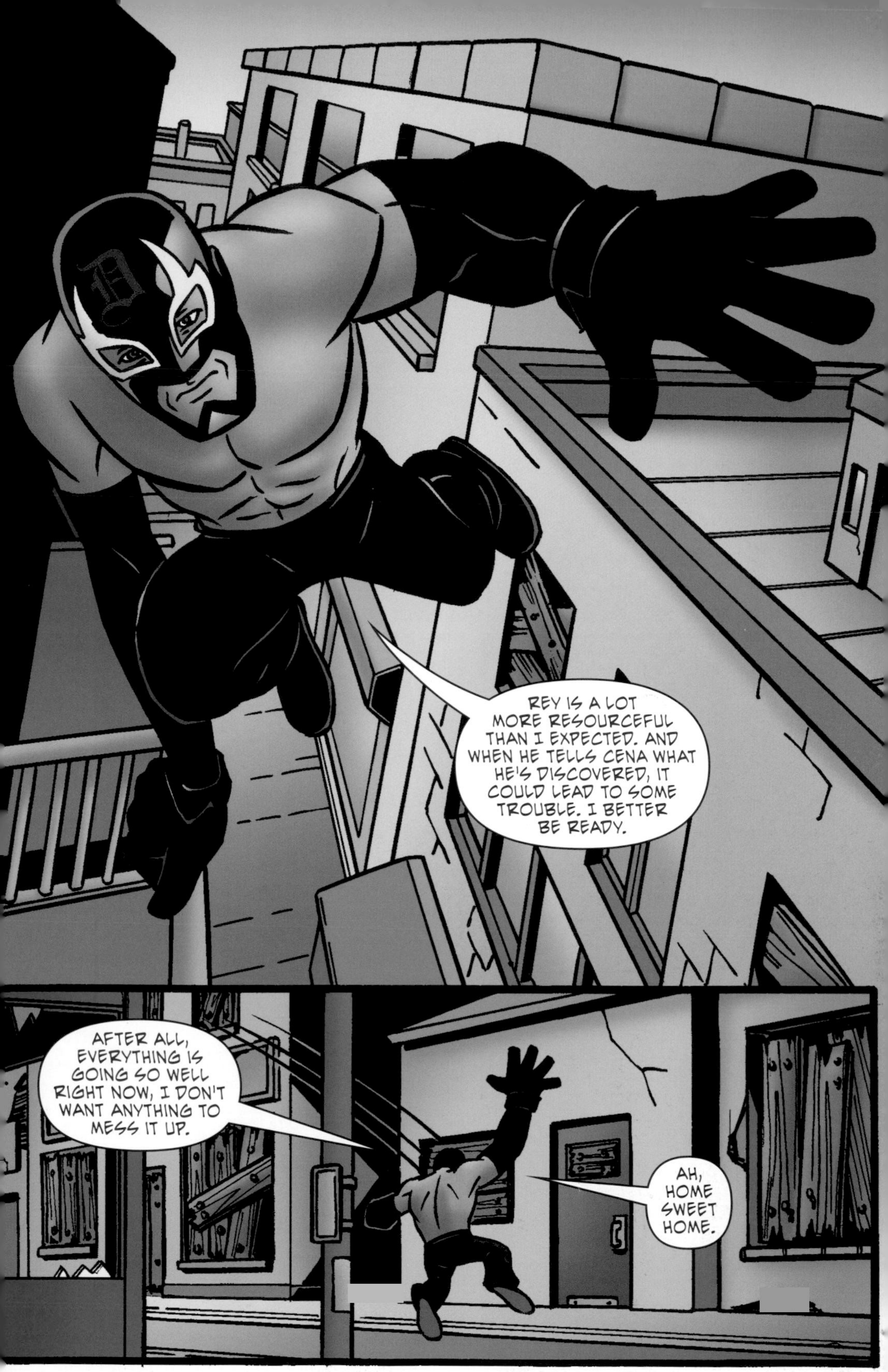
REY IS A LOT MORE RESOURCEFUL THAN I EXPECTED. AND WHEN HE TELLS CENA WHAT HE'S DISCOVERED, IT COULD LEAD TO SOME TROUBLE. I BETTER BE READY.
AFTER ALL, EVERYTHING IS GOING SO WELL RIGHT NOW, I DON'T WANT ANYTHING TO MESS IT UP.
AH, HOME SWEET HOME.

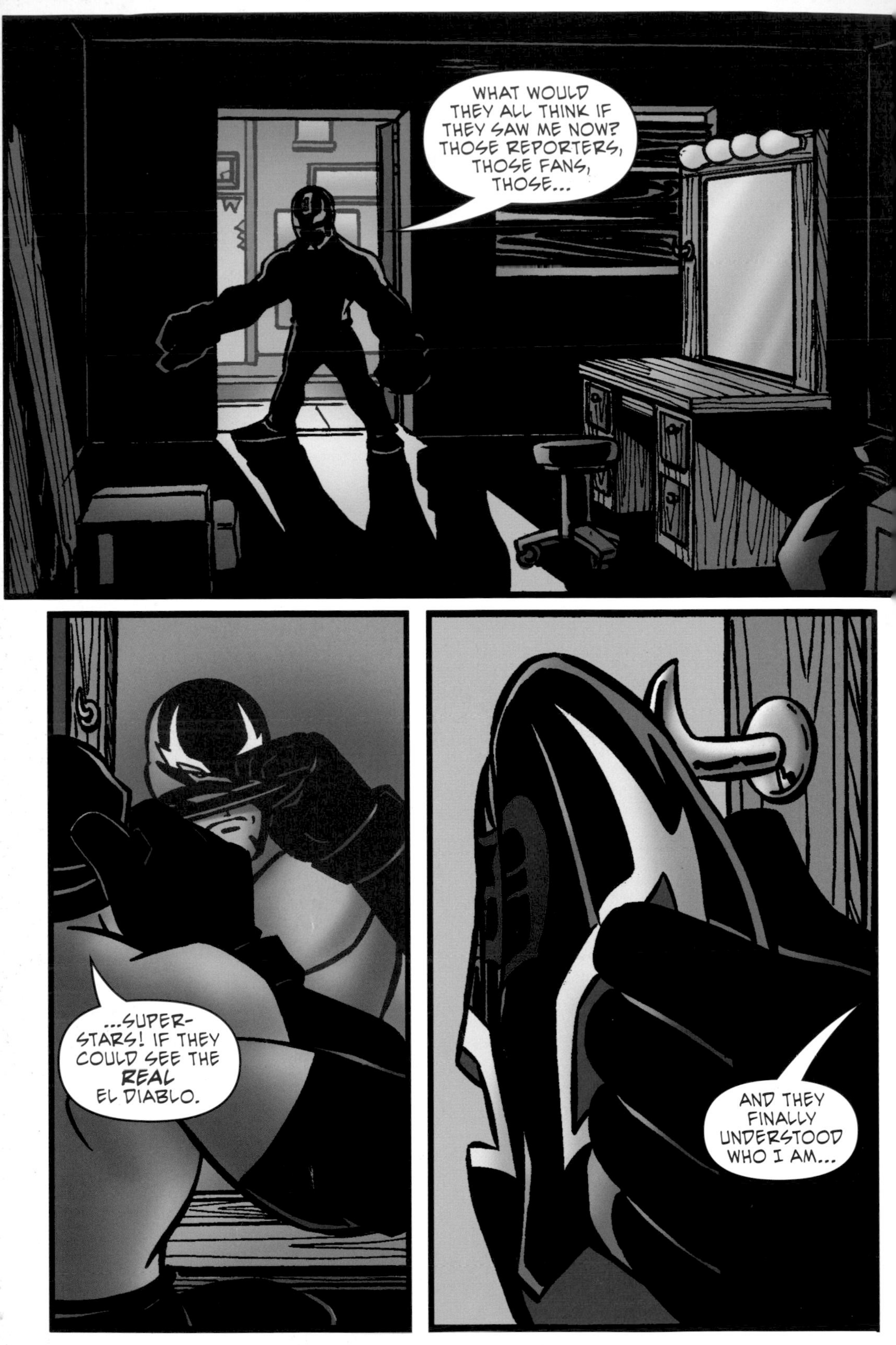
WHAT WOULD THEY ALL THINK IF THEY SAW ME NOW? THOSE REPORTERS, THOSE FANS, THOSE...
...SUPER-STARS! IF THEY COULD SEE THE REAL EL DIABLO.
AND THEY FINALLY UNDERSTOOD WHO I AM...

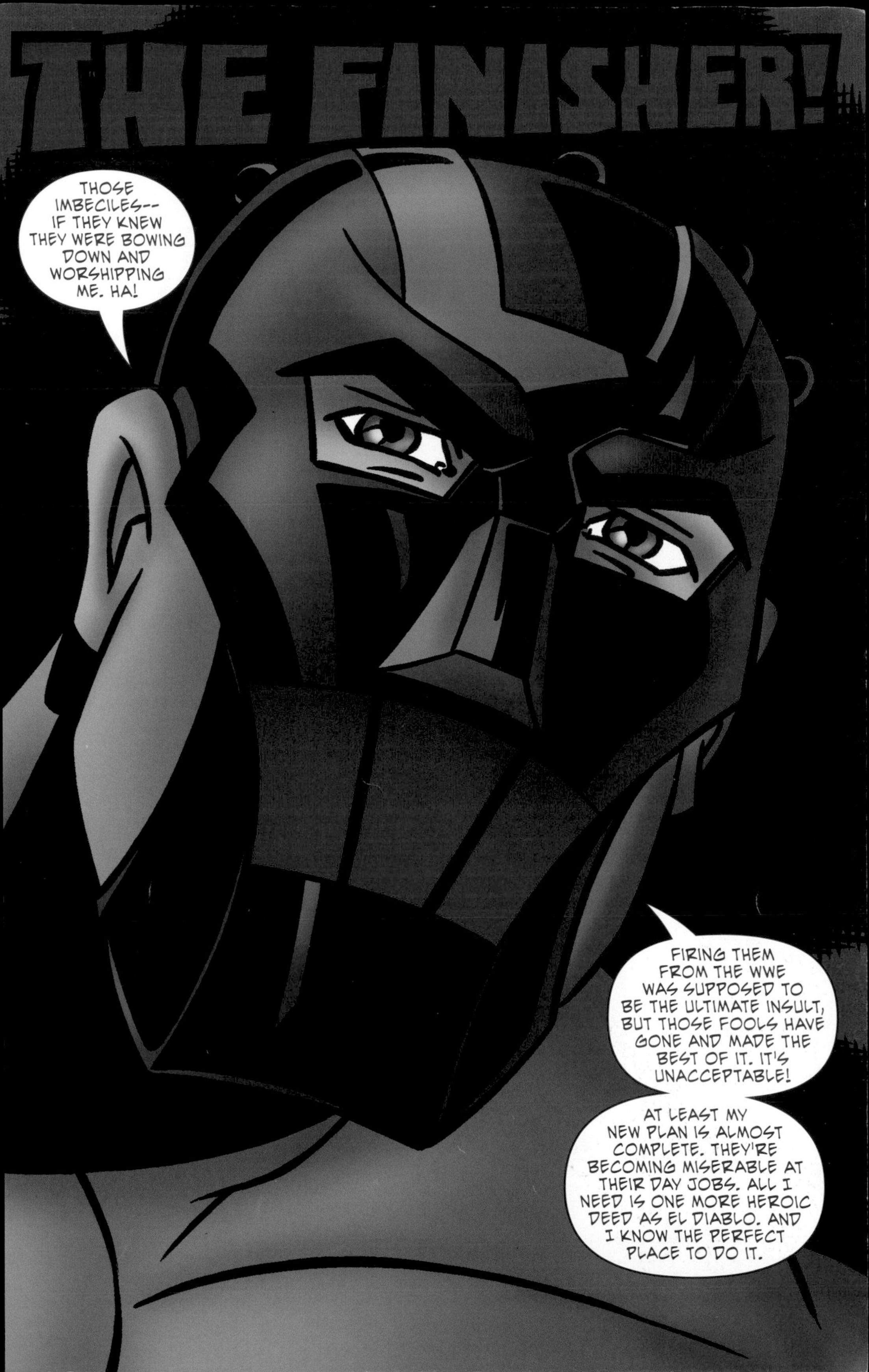
THE FINISHER!
THOSE IMBECILES-- IF THEY KNEW THEY WERE BOWING DOWN AND WORSHIPPING ME. HA!
FIRING THEM FROM THE WWE WAS SUPPOSED TO BE THE ULTIMATE INSULT, BUT THOSE FOOLS HAVE GONE AND MADE THE BEST OF IT. IT'S UNACCEPTABLE!
AT LEAST MY NEW PLAN IS ALMOST COMPLETE. THEY'RE BECOMING MISERABLE AT THEIR DAY JOBS. ALL I NEED IS ONE MORE HEROIC DEED AS EL DIABLO. AND I KNOW THE PERFECT PLACE TO DO IT.

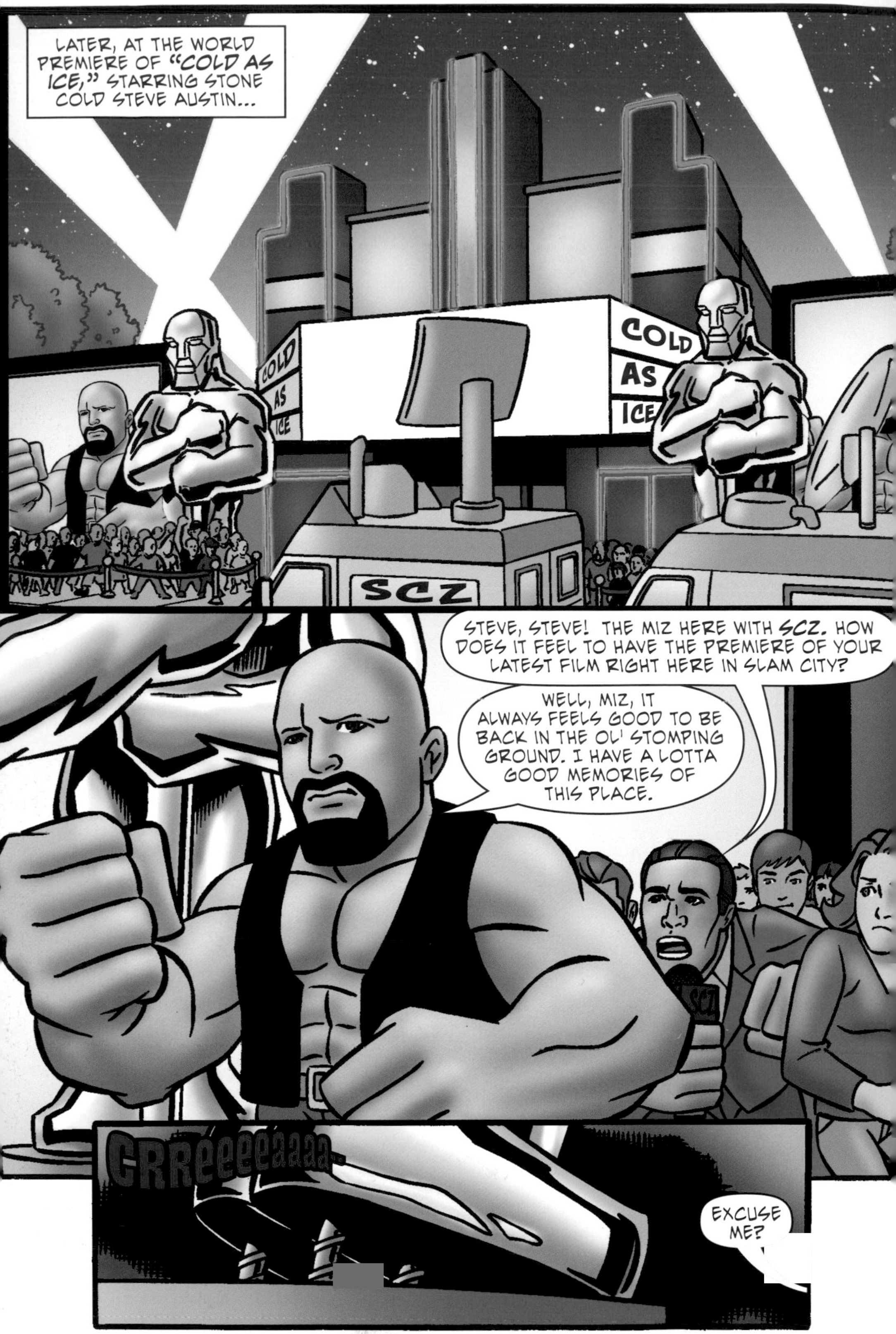

LATER, AT THE WORLD PREMIERE OF "COLD AS ICE," STARRING STONE COLD STEVE AUSTIN...
COLD AS ICE
COLD AS ICE
SCZ
STEVE, STEVE! THE MIZ HERE WITH SCZ. HOW DOES IT FEEL TO HAVE THE PREMIERE OF YOUR LATEST FILM RIGHT HERE IN SLAM CITY?
WELL, MIZ, IT ALWAYS FEELS GOOD TO BE BACK IN THE OL' STOMPING GROUND. I HAVE A LOTTA GOOD MEMORIES OF THIS PLACE.
GRReeeeaaaa-
EXCUSE ME?

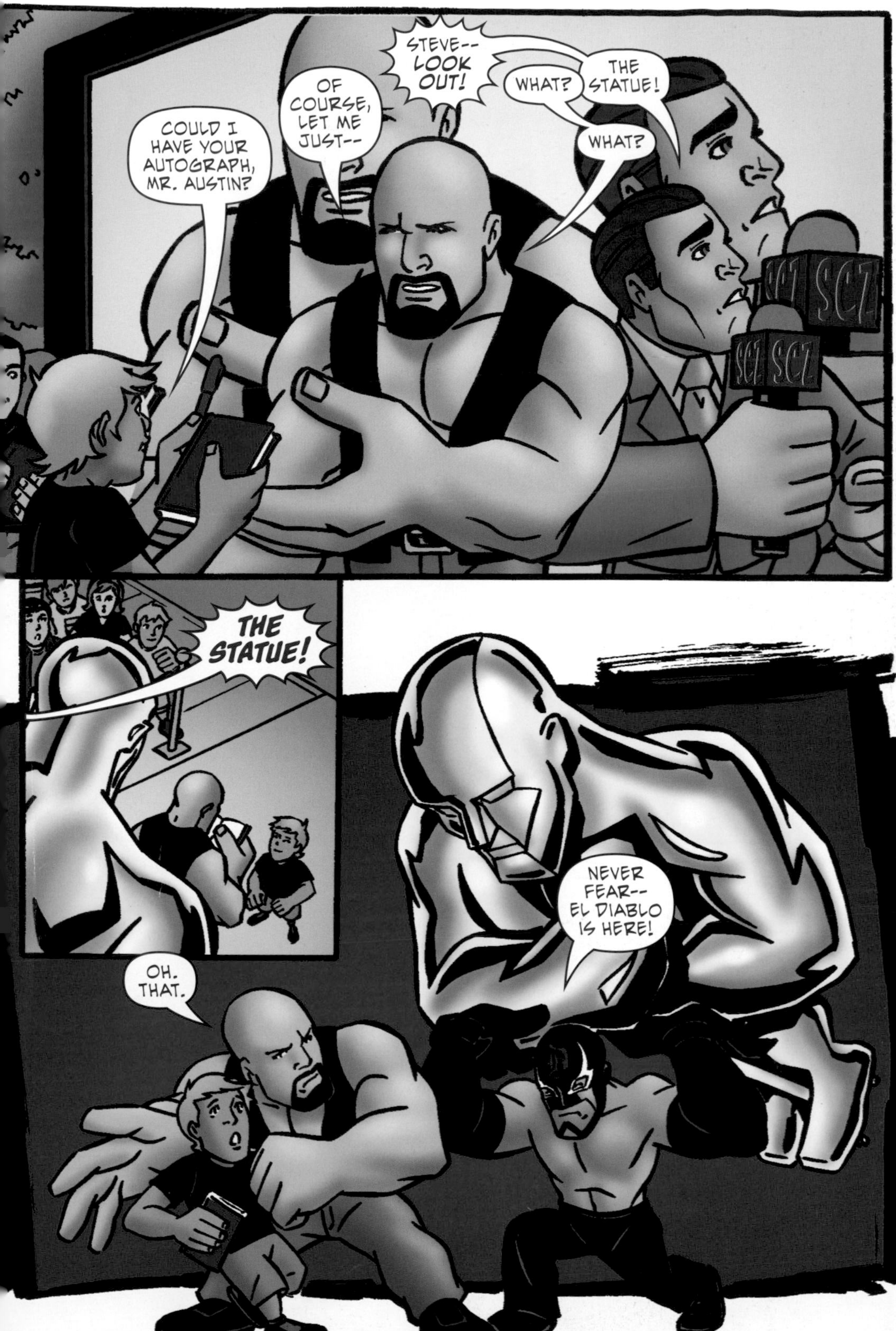
COULD I HAVE YOUR AUTOGRAPH, MR. AUSTIN?
OF COURSE, LET ME JUST--
STEVE-- LOOK OUT!
WHAT?
THE STATUE!
WHAT?
SCZ
THE STATUE!
NEVER FEAR-- EL DIABLO IS HERE!
OH. THAT.

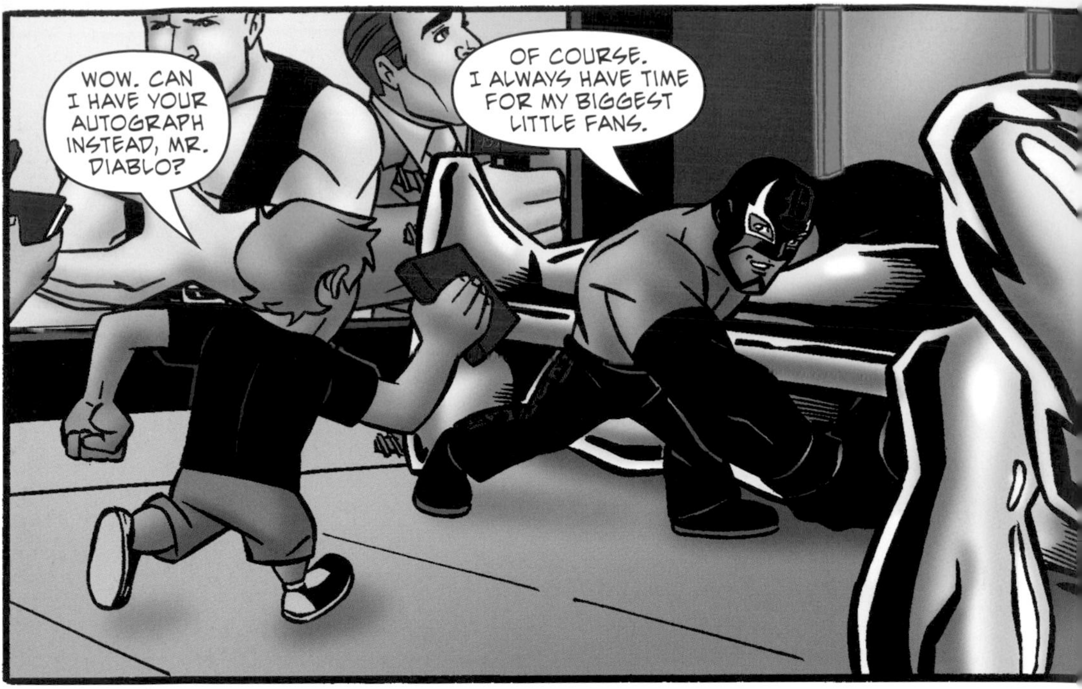
WOW. CAN I HAVE YOUR AUTOGRAPH INSTEAD, MR. DIABLO?
OF COURSE. I ALWAYS HAVE TIME FOR MY BIGGEST LITTLE FANS.

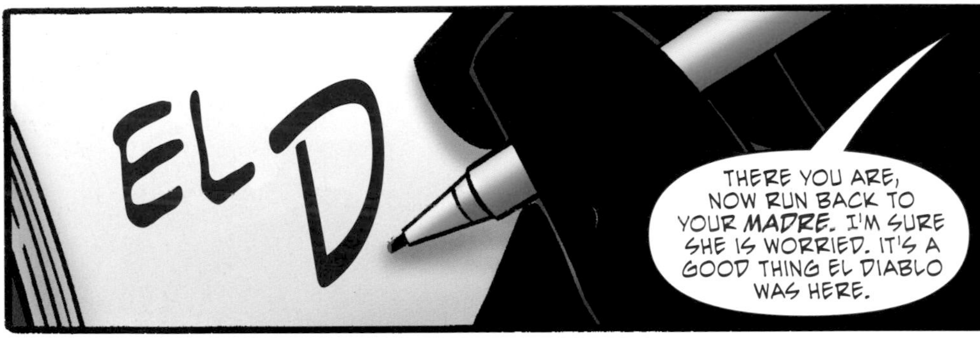
EL D
THERE YOU ARE, NOW RUN BACK TO YOUR ***MADRE***. I'M SURE SHE IS WORRIED. IT'S A GOOD THING EL DIABLO WAS HERE.

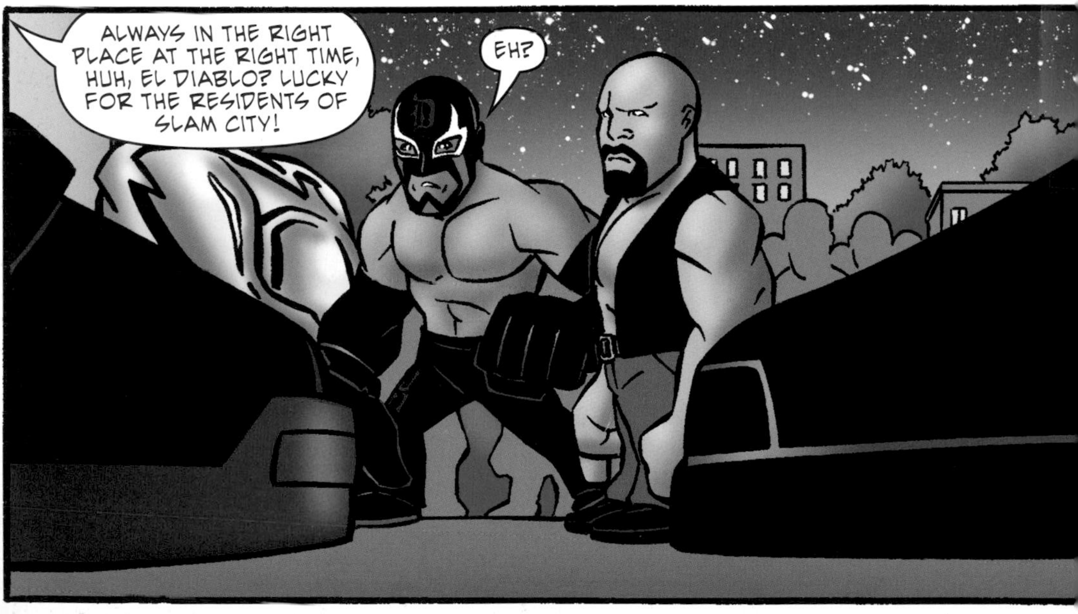
ALWAYS IN THE RIGHT PLACE AT THE RIGHT TIME, HUH, EL DIABLO? LUCKY FOR THE RESIDENTS OF SLAM CITY!
EH?

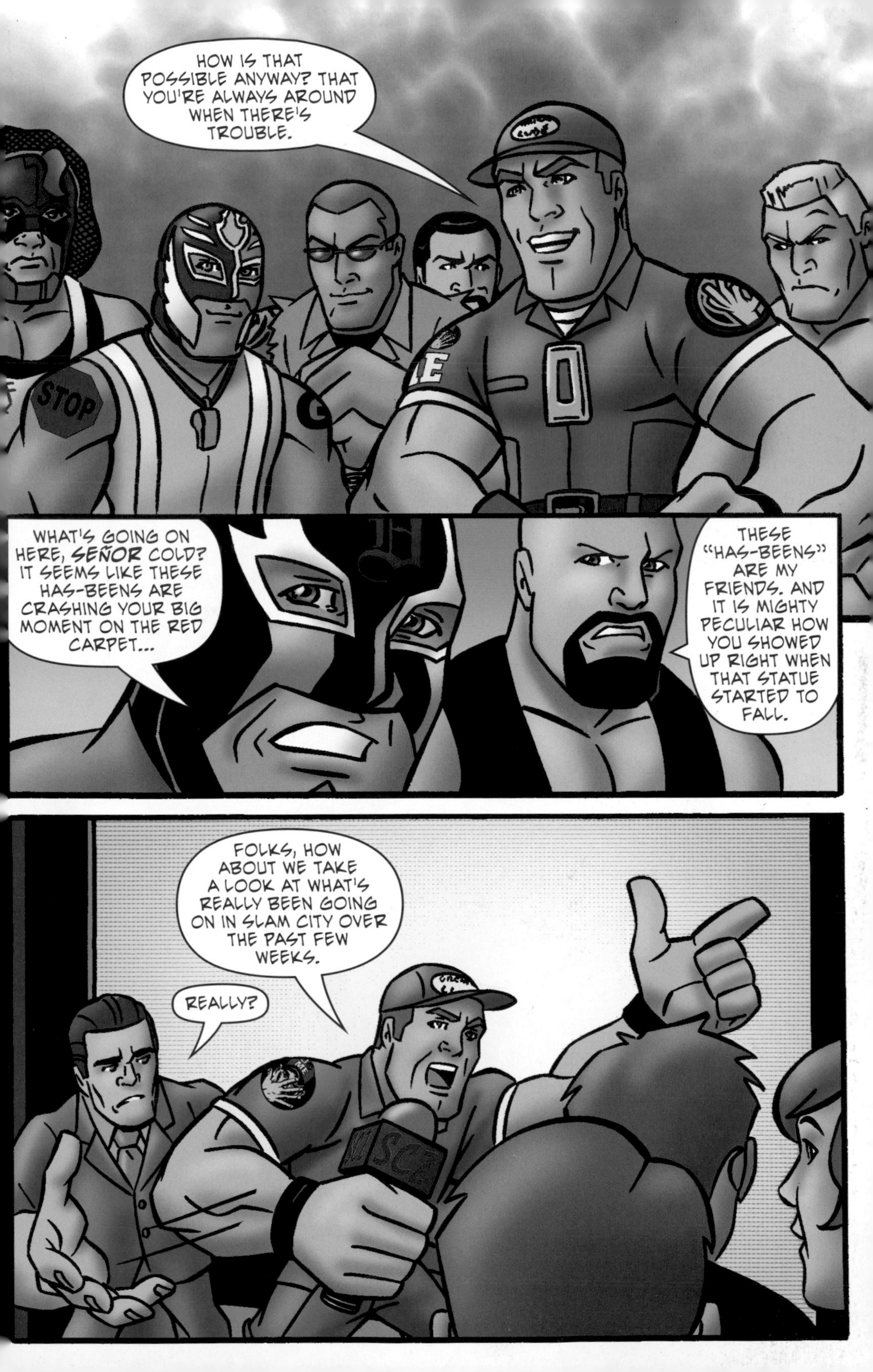
HOW IS THAT POSSIBLE ANYWAY? THAT YOU'RE ALWAYS AROUND WHEN THERE'S TROUBLE.
STOP
WHAT'S GOING ON HERE, SEÑOR COLD? IT SEEMS LIKE THESE HAS-BEENS ARE CRASHING YOUR BIG MOMENT ON THE RED CARPET...
THESE "HAS-BEENS" ARE MY FRIENDS. AND IT IS MIGHTY PECULIAR HOW YOU SHOWED UP RIGHT WHEN THAT STATUE STARTED TO FALL.
FOLKS, HOW ABOUT WE TAKE A LOOK AT WHAT'S REALLY BEEN GOING ON IN SLAM CITY OVER THE PAST FEW WEEKS.
REALLY?

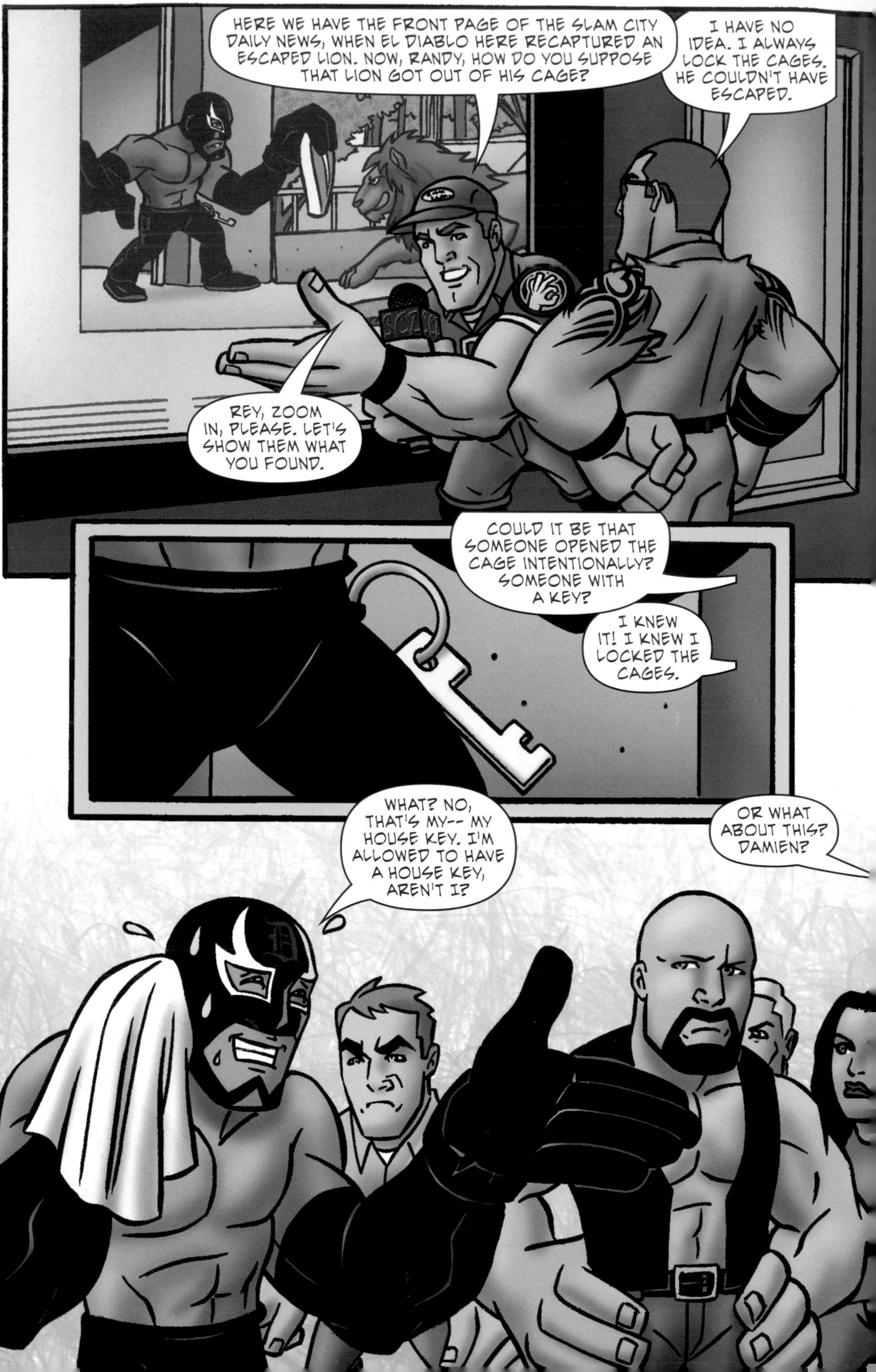
HERE WE HAVE THE FRONT PAGE OF THE SLAM CITY DAILY NEWS, WHEN EL DIABLO HERE RECAPTURED AN ESCAPED LION. NOW, RANDY, HOW DO YOU SUPPOSE THAT LION GOT OUT OF HIS CAGE?
I HAVE NO IDEA. I ALWAYS LOCK THE CAGES. HE COULDN'T HAVE ESCAPED.
REY, ZOOM IN, PLEASE. LET'S SHOW THEM WHAT YOU FOUND.
COULD IT BE THAT SOMEONE OPENED THE CAGE INTENTIONALLY? SOMEONE WITH A KEY?
I KNEW IT! I KNEW I LOCKED THE CAGES.
WHAT? NO, THAT'S MY-- MY HOUSE KEY. I'M ALLOWED TO HAVE A HOUSE KEY, AREN'T I?
OR WHAT ABOUT THIS? DAMIEN?

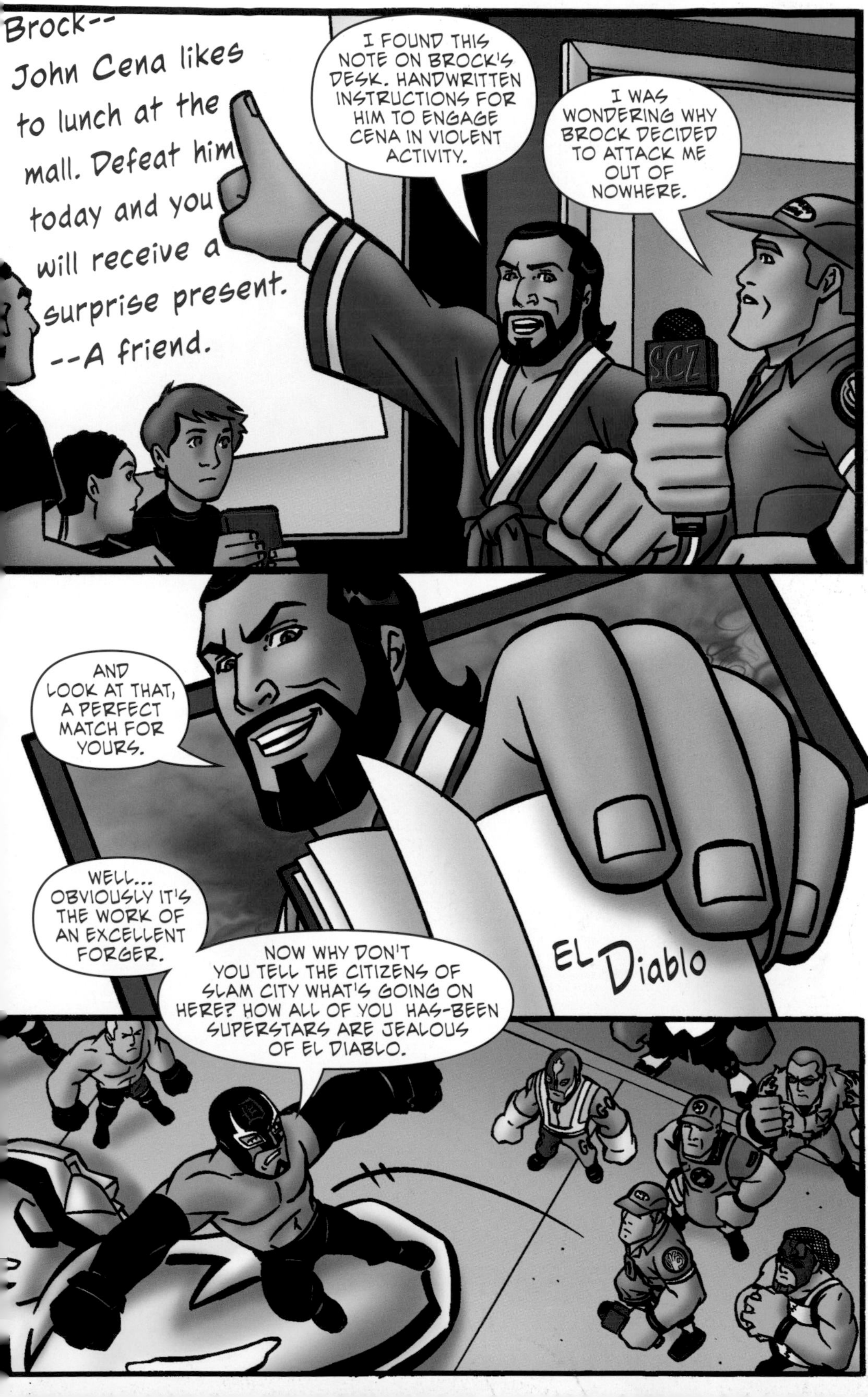
Brock--
John Cena likes to lunch at the mall. Defeat him today and you will receive a surprise present.
--A friend.
I FOUND THIS NOTE ON BROCK'S DESK. HANDWRITTEN INSTRUCTIONS FOR HIM TO ENGAGE CENA IN VIOLENT ACTIVITY.
I WAS WONDERING WHY BROCK DECIDED TO ATTACK ME OUT OF NOWHERE.
SCZ
AND LOOK AT THAT, A PERFECT MATCH FOR YOURS.
EL Diablo
WELL... OBVIOUSLY IT'S THE WORK OF AN EXCELLENT FORGER.
NOW WHY DON'T YOU TELL THE CITIZENS OF SLAM CITY WHAT'S GOING ON HERE? HOW ALL OF YOU HAS-BEEN SUPERSTARS ARE JEALOUS OF EL DIABLO.

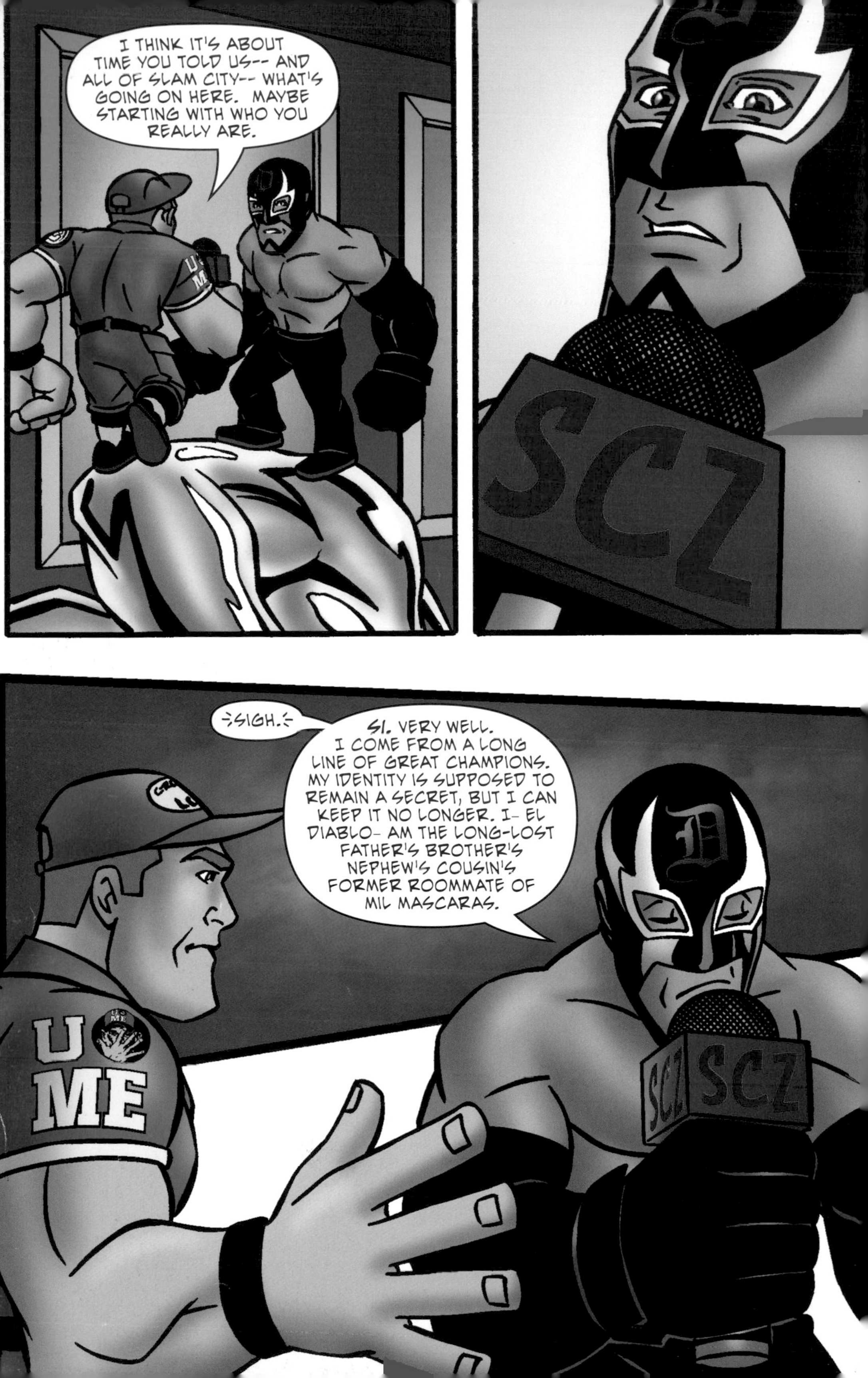
I THINK IT'S ABOUT TIME YOU TOLD US-- AND ALL OF SLAM CITY-- WHAT'S GOING ON HERE. MAYBE STARTING WITH WHO YOU REALLY ARE.
SCZ
-SIGH.-
SI. VERY WELL. I COME FROM A LONG LINE OF GREAT CHAMPIONS. MY IDENTITY IS SUPPOSED TO REMAIN A SECRET, BUT I CAN KEEP IT NO LONGER. I- EL DIABLO- AM THE LONG-LOST FATHER'S BROTHER'S NEPHEW'S COUSIN'S FORMER ROOMMATE OF MIL MASCARAS.
U ME
SCZ SCZ

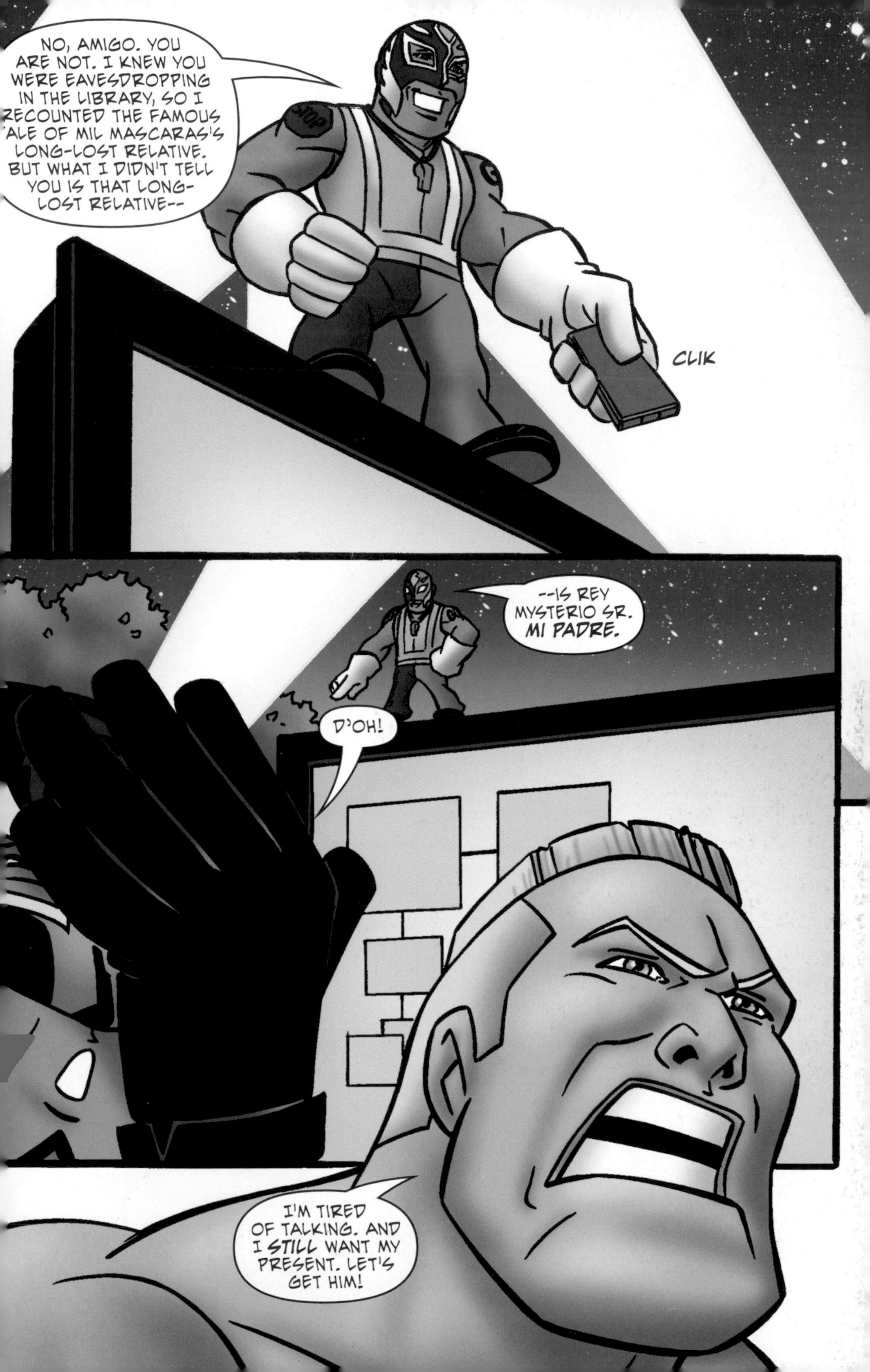
NO, AMIGO. YOU ARE NOT. I KNEW YOU WERE EAVESDROPPING IN THE LIBRARY, SO I RECOUNTED THE FAMOUS TALE OF MIL MASCARAS'S LONG-LOST RELATIVE. BUT WHAT I DIDN'T TELL YOU IS THAT LONG-LOST RELATIVE--
CLIK
--IS REY MYSTERIO SR. MI PADRE.
D'OH!
I'M TIRED OF TALKING. AND I STILL WANT MY PRESENT. LET'S GET HIM!

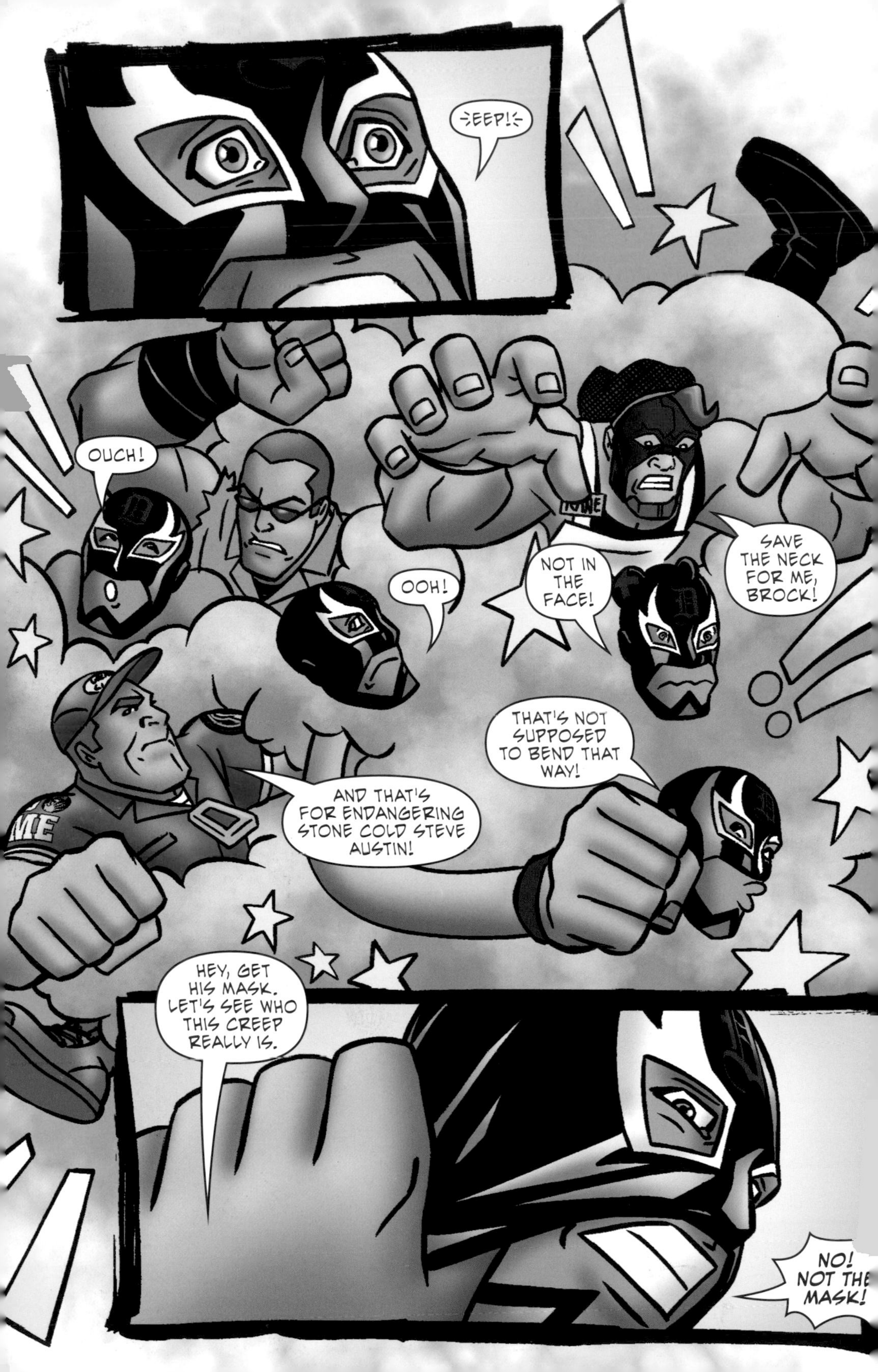
EEP!
OUCH!
OOH!
NOT IN THE FACE!
SAVE THE NECK FOR ME, BROCK!
THAT'S NOT SUPPOSED TO BEND THAT WAY!
AND THAT'S FOR ENDANGERING STONE COLD STEVE AUSTIN!
HEY, GET HIS MASK. LET'S SEE WHO THIS CREEP REALLY IS.
NO! NOT THE MASK!

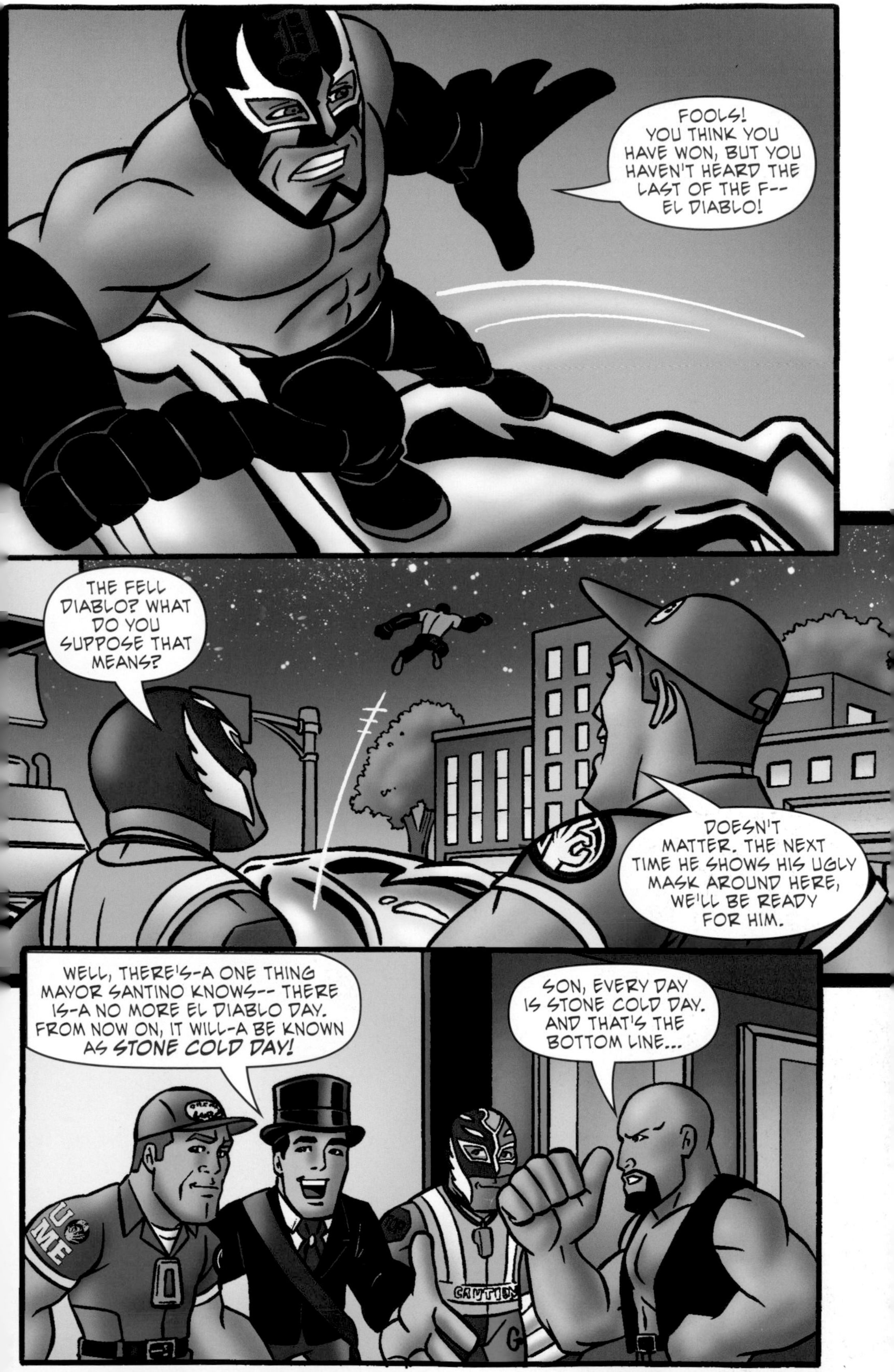
FOOLS! YOU THINK YOU HAVE WON, BUT YOU HAVEN'T HEARD THE LAST OF THE F-- EL DIABLO!
THE FELL DIABLO? WHAT DO YOU SUPPOSE THAT MEANS?
DOESN'T MATTER. THE NEXT TIME HE SHOWS HIS UGLY MASK AROUND HERE, WE'LL BE READY FOR HIM.
WELL, THERE'S-A ONE THING MAYOR SANTINO KNOWS-- THERE IS-A NO MORE EL DIABLO DAY. FROM NOW ON, IT WILL-A BE KNOWN AS STONE COLD DAY!
SON, EVERY DAY IS STONE COLD DAY. AND THAT'S THE BOTTOM LINE...

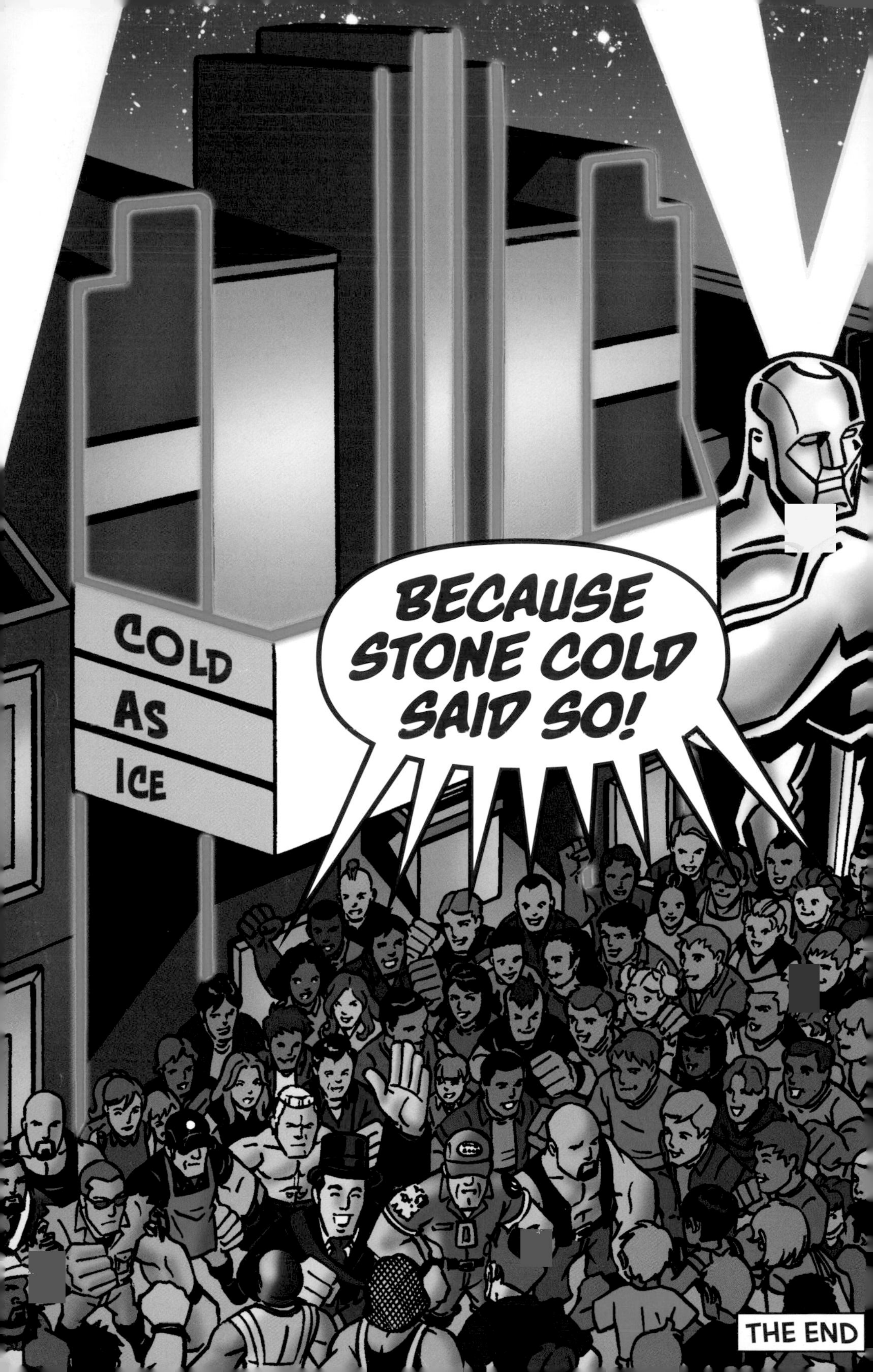
COLD AS ICE
BECAUSE STONE COLD SAID SO!
THE END

WATCH OUT FOR PAPERCUTZ™

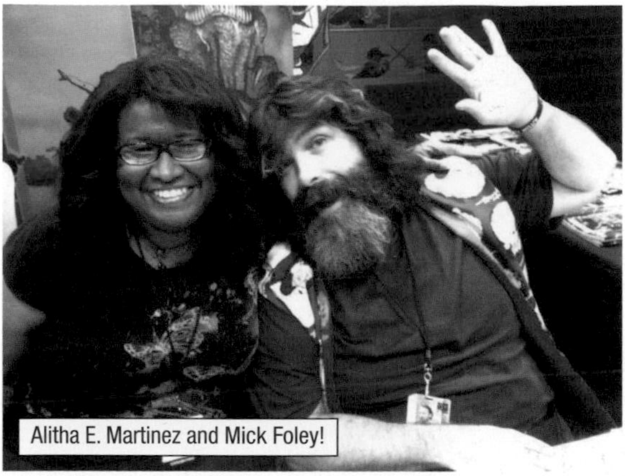
Alitha E. Martinez and Mick Foley!

Welcome to the slammin' and bangin' second WWE SLAM CITY graphic novel from Papercutz, those blue pencil-neck geeks who are dedicated to publishing great graphic novels for all ages! And me? Your Editor-in-Chief, from New York City, at a height of 6'1", weighing 250 lbs... the World's Nerdiest Comicbook Editor... JIM SALICRUP!

Let me tell you something, brother... and sister... the WWE SUPERSTARS are here! Not just in the awesome WWE SLAM CITY graphic novel you're looking at right now, but in a series of comics and graphic novels published by the Papercutz imprint, Super Genius! Here's how it works, first four comics are published featuring one colossal story, and then that story is collected into a pulse-pounding paperback edition. The first eight comics and the first two graphic novels are fast becoming hot collectors' items and here's why: Unlike other graphic novels that are reprinted endlessly, these two graphic novels may never be published again in their original form. If they ever are republished—it'll be with re-worked stories and without every single WWE Superstar in the current editions. So, consider yourself warned, that once "WWE SUPERSTARS #1 "Money in the Bank" and WWE SUPERSTARS #2 "Haze of Glory" go out of print, that's it! The only way you'll be able to get them is at comicstores as back issues.

And just in case you've got here late, here's the rundown on what is featured in those comics and graphic novels...

WWE SUPERSTARS #1 "Money in the Bank" is written by Mick Foley (with Shane Riches)! That's right—Mick Foley, a member of the WWE Hall of Fame! That Mick Foley! The man who was Dude Love, Cactus Jack, and Mankind! But also the Mick Foley who is also a New York Times best-selling author, who has written memoirs, novels, and children's books. "Money in the Bank" is also illustrated by Alitha E. Martinez, the artist who has drawn every WWE SLAM CITY graphic novel so far! But "Money in the Bank" is all about a different, darker, grimmer city called Titan City. It is there where John Cena has been falsely convicted of stealing $10,000,000.00. The Authority wants their money back, and John Cena wants to find out who set him up and why. It's a classic crime thriller—except everyone in the story is a WWE Superstar. Over 25 WWE Superstars, as you've never seen them before! (And just to make this graphic novel even more irresistible—it's only $9.99!)

WWE SUPERSTARS #2 "Haze of Glory" is co-created by Mick Foley and Shane Riches, and illustrated by Puste (featuring guest artists Alitha E. Martinez, Miran Kim, and Fred Harper). Now for something completely different—a comedy/adventure starring the WWE Superstars! When four WWE Superstars seemingly go insane and wreck a taping of WWE RAW, Mr. McMahon wants an explanation from them or else they're fired! The one problem is that none of the accused WWE Superstars can remember what happened—especially Daniel Bryan! He thinks he was a knight in a Lord of the Rings-like world, battling dragons and apes! Featuring special appearances from Mankind and the Immortal Hulk Hogan, and many others, this is one WWE adventure that YOU won't forget!

And just when you thought it couldn't get any stranger or far-out, along comes WWE SUPERSTARS #3 "Legends!" co-created by Mick Foley and Shane Riches, illustrated by Paris Cullins, featuring every dream match you ever, well, dreamed about! But none of the matches are in a traditional ring. Instead they're taking place in the most unlikely places imaginable—such as an ancient coliseum, a pirate ship, and even on the planet Mars! With over twice as many WWE Superstars and WWE Legends as "Money in the Bank," you'll never know who'll be popping up next in the pages of "Legends!" Don't take our word for it—check out the short sneak peak on the following pages! But we warn you, you'll want to get the whole story as soon as you finish these few pages!

Speaking of WWE collectors' items—it looks like WWE SLAM CITY may become one as well! This could be the final WWE SLAM CITY graphic novel ever. Does that mean we'll never learn the final fate of The Finisher? Will the WWE Superstars never get their jobs back? Check out the animated episodes online or on the WWE Network, and keep an eye on the WWE SUPERSTAR graphic novels—you may never know what to expect there!

So until next time, in the words of the Immortal Hulk Hogan, "To all my little Hulkamaniacs, say your prayers, take your vitamins, and you will never go wrong."

Thanks,

Jim

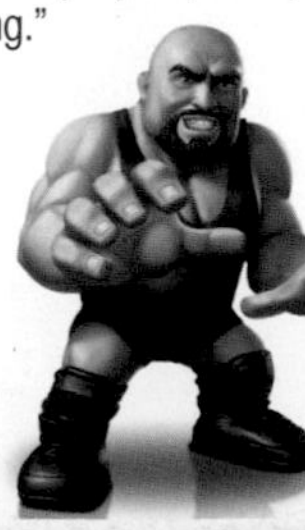

STAY IN TOUCH!

EMAIL:	salicrup@papercutz.com
WEB:	papercutz.com
TWITTER:	@papercutzgn
FACEBOOK:	PAPERCUTZGRAPHICNOVELS
FAN MAIL:	Papercutz, 160 Broadway, Suite 700, East Wing, New York, NY 10038

R E A D

RELIVE · EXPLORE · ADVENTURE · DISCOVER

IT'S PASS GO TIME!

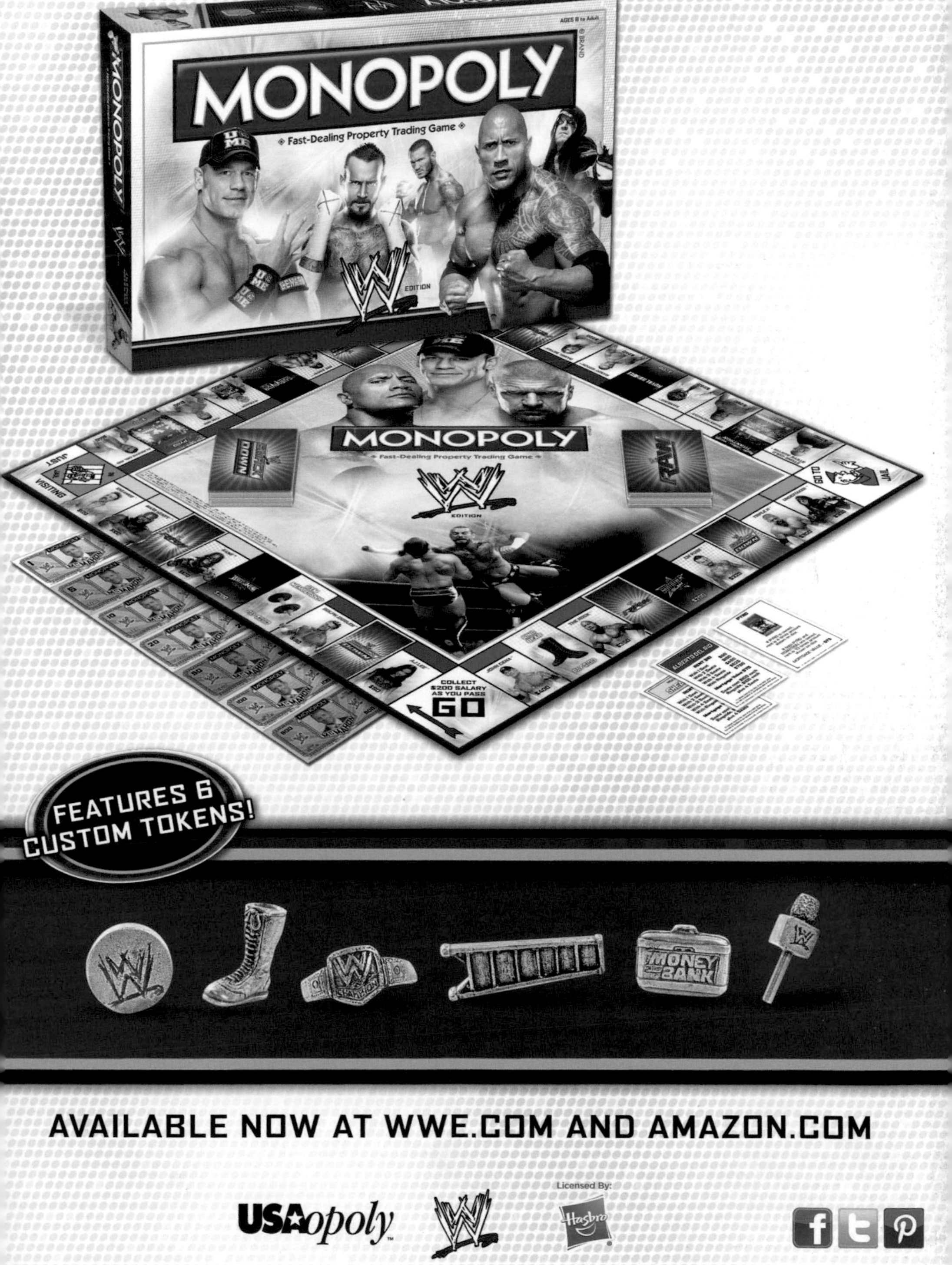
MONOPOLY
Fast-Dealing Property Trading Game
EDITION
AGES 8 to Adult
COLLECT $200 SALARY AS YOU PASS GO
JUST VISITING
GO TO JAIL
FEATURES 6 CUSTOM TOKENS!
MONEY IN THE BANK

AVAILABLE NOW AT WWE.COM AND AMAZON.COM

USAopoly

Licensed By: Hasbro

Special Sneak Peak at WWE SUPERSTARS #3 "Legends!"

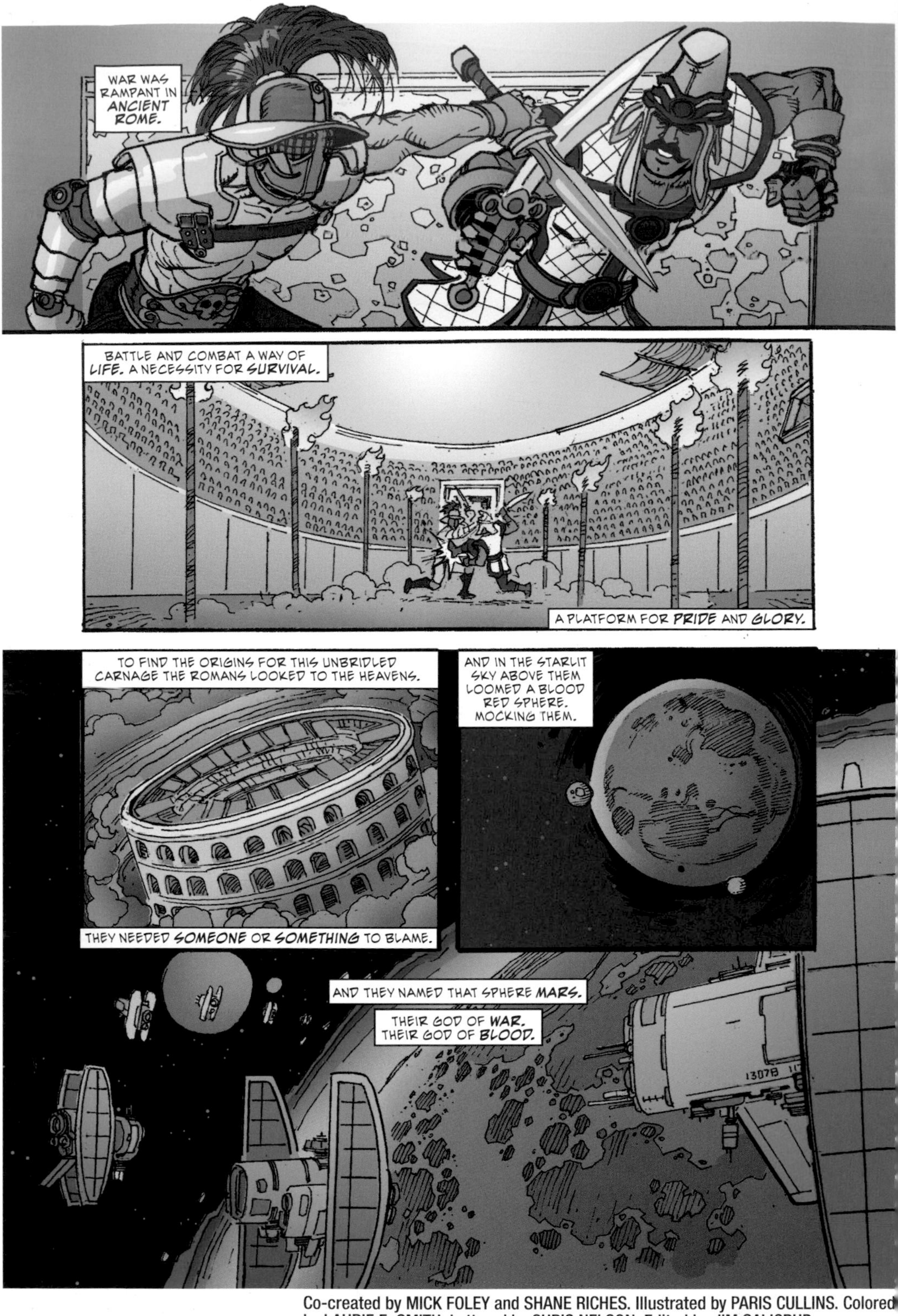

WAR WAS RAMPANT IN ANCIENT ROME.
BATTLE AND COMBAT A WAY OF LIFE. A NECESSITY FOR SURVIVAL.
A PLATFORM FOR PRIDE AND GLORY.
TO FIND THE ORIGINS FOR THIS UNBRIDLED CARNAGE THE ROMANS LOOKED TO THE HEAVENS.
THEY NEEDED SOMEONE OR SOMETHING TO BLAME.
AND IN THE STARLIT SKY ABOVE THEM LOOMED A BLOOD RED SPHERE. MOCKING THEM.
AND THEY NAMED THAT SPHERE MARS.
THEIR GOD OF WAR. THEIR GOD OF BLOOD.
1307B

Co-created by MICK FOLEY and SHANE RICHES. Illustrated by PARIS CULLINS. Colored by LAURIE E. SMITH. Lettered by CHRIS NELSON. Edited by JIM SALICRUP.

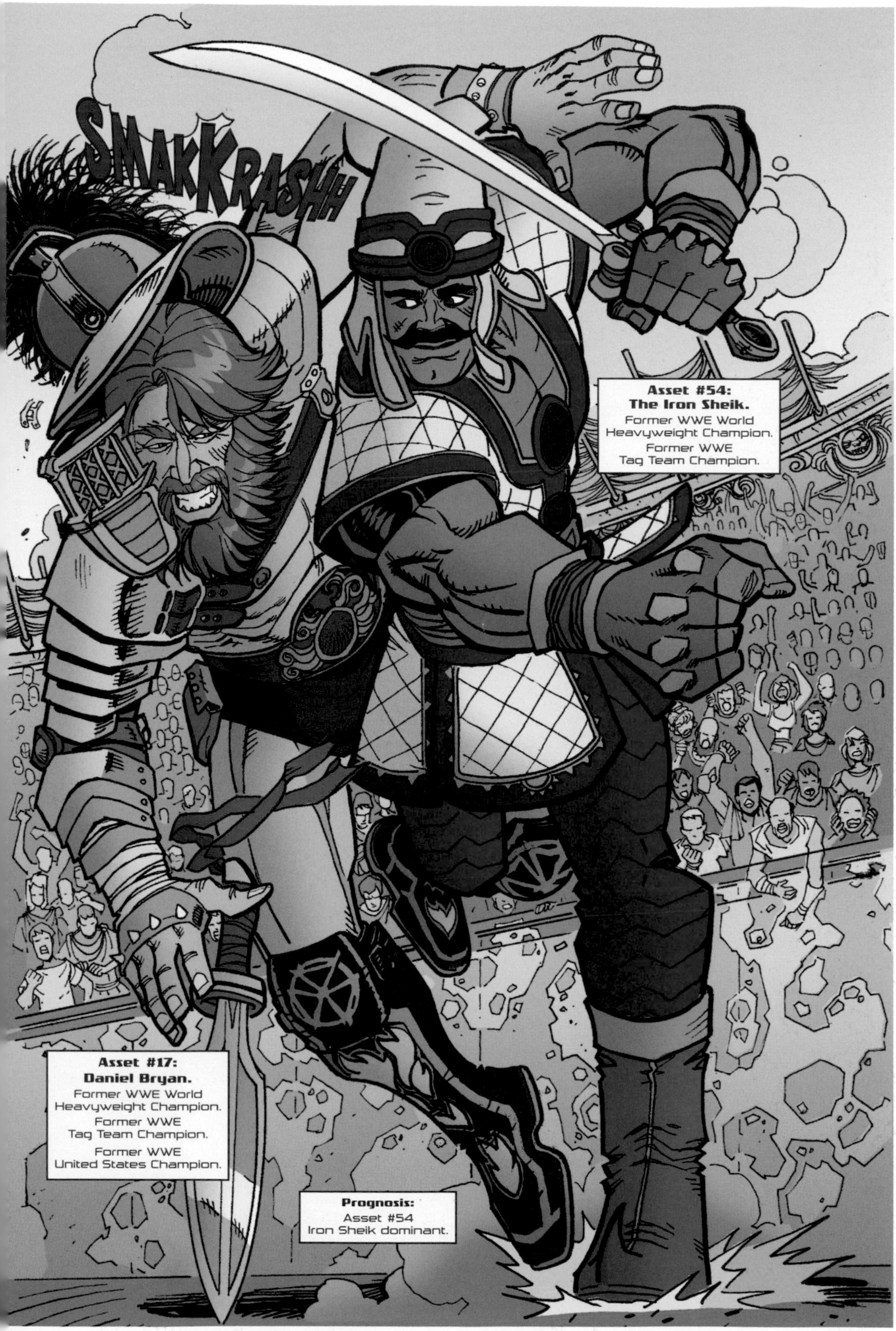
SMAKKRASHH
Asset #54: The Iron Sheik.
Former WWE World Heavyweight Champion.
Former WWE Tag Team Champion.
Asset #17: Daniel Bryan.
Former WWE World Heavyweight Champion.
Former WWE Tag Team Champion.
Former WWE United States Champion.
Prognosis: Asset #54 Iron Sheik dominant.

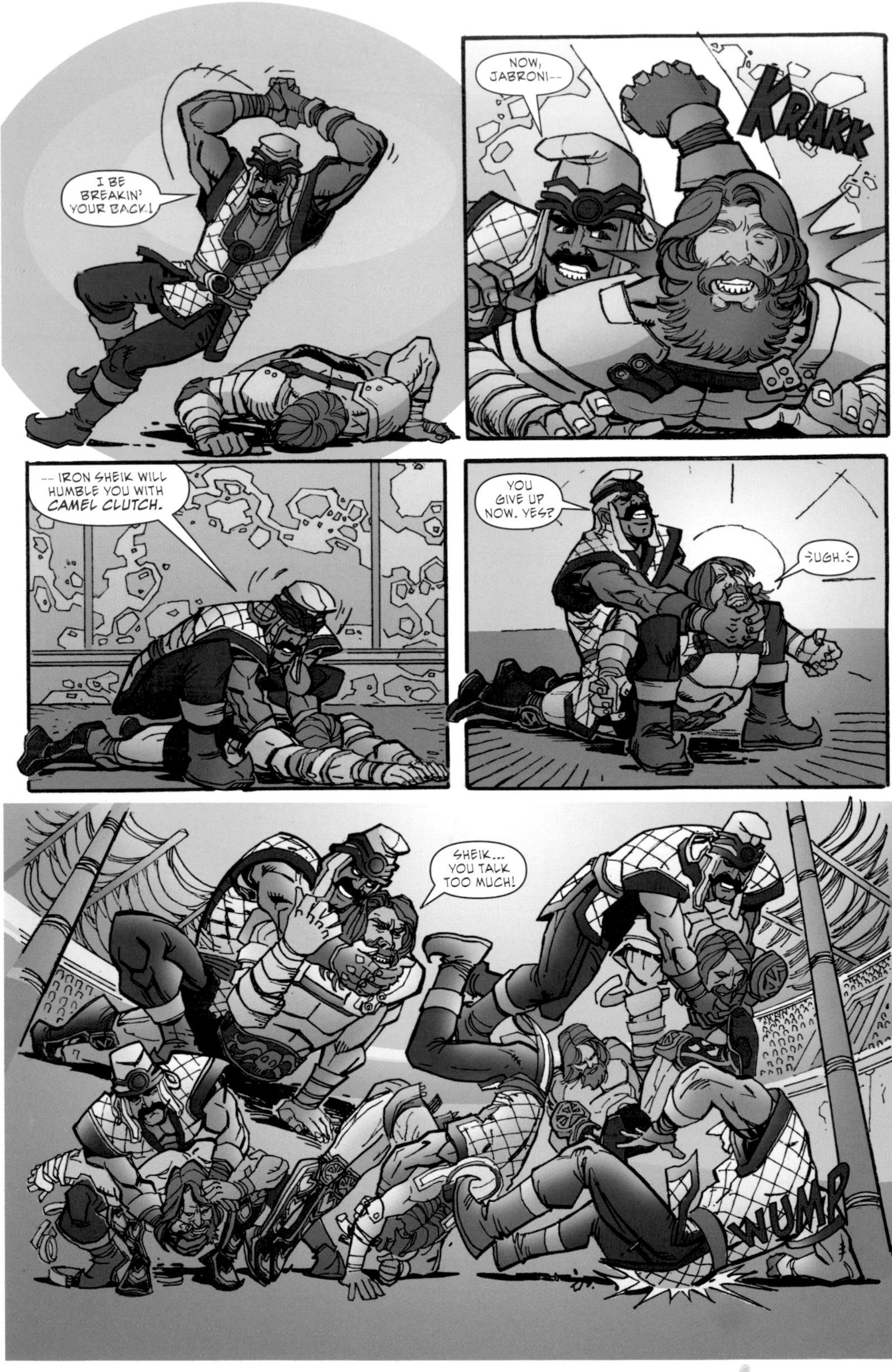
I BE BREAKIN' YOUR BACK!
NOW, JABRONI--
KRAKK
--IRON SHEIK WILL HUMBLE YOU WITH CAMEL CLUTCH.
YOU GIVE UP NOW. YES?
UGH.
SHEIK... YOU TALK TOO MUCH!
WUMP

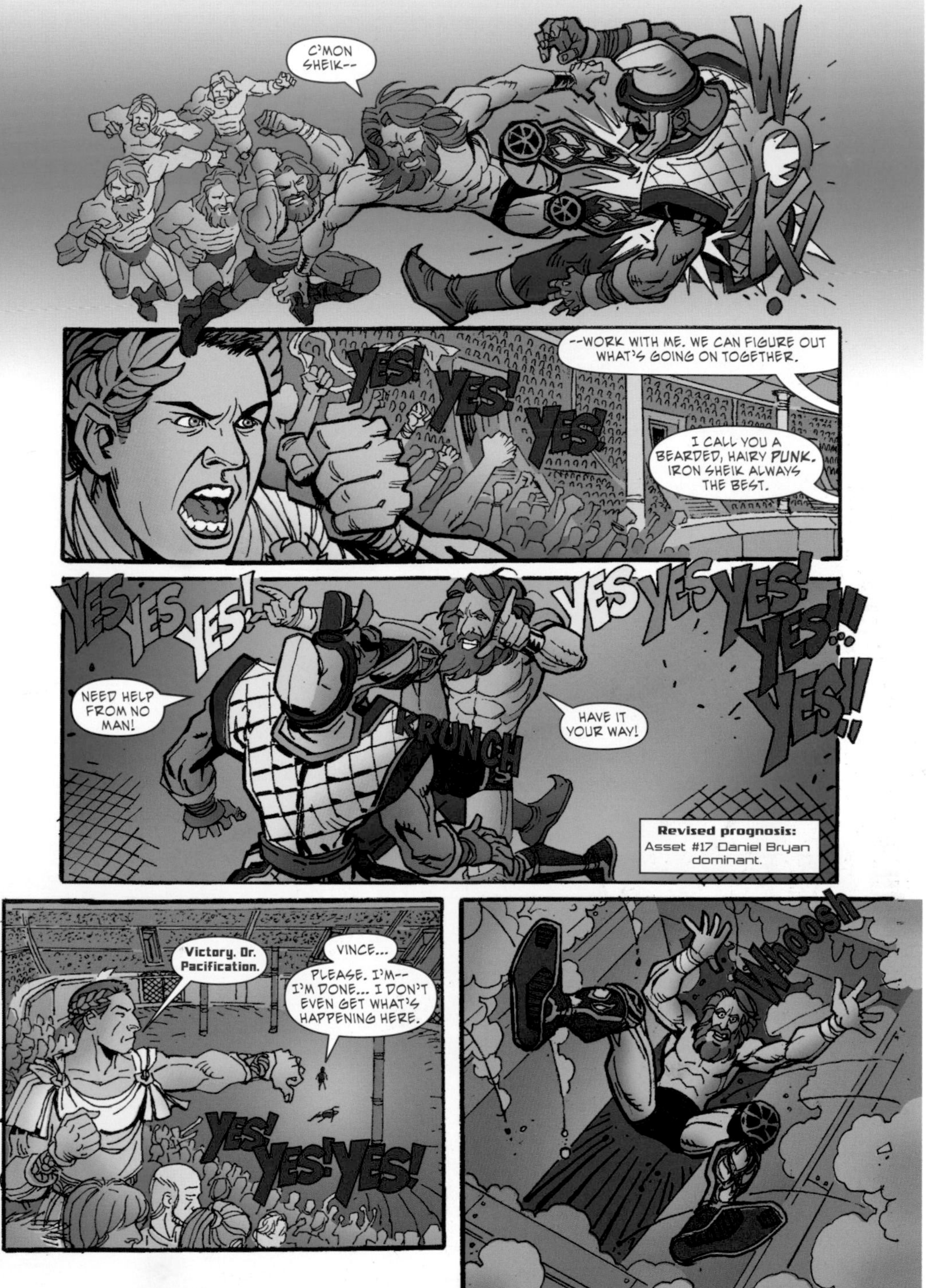
C'MON SHEIK--
WOK!
--WORK WITH ME. WE CAN FIGURE OUT WHAT'S GOING ON TOGETHER.
YES! YES! YES!
I CALL YOU A BEARDED, HAIRY PUNK. IRON SHEIK ALWAYS THE BEST.
YES YES YES!
NEED HELP FROM NO MAN!
KRUNCH
HAVE IT YOUR WAY!
YES YES YES! YES!! YES!!
Revised prognosis:
Asset #17 Daniel Bryan dominant.
Victory. Or. Pacification.
VINCE...
PLEASE. I'M-- I'M DONE... I DON'T EVEN GET WHAT'S HAPPENING HERE.
YES! YES! YES!
Whoosh

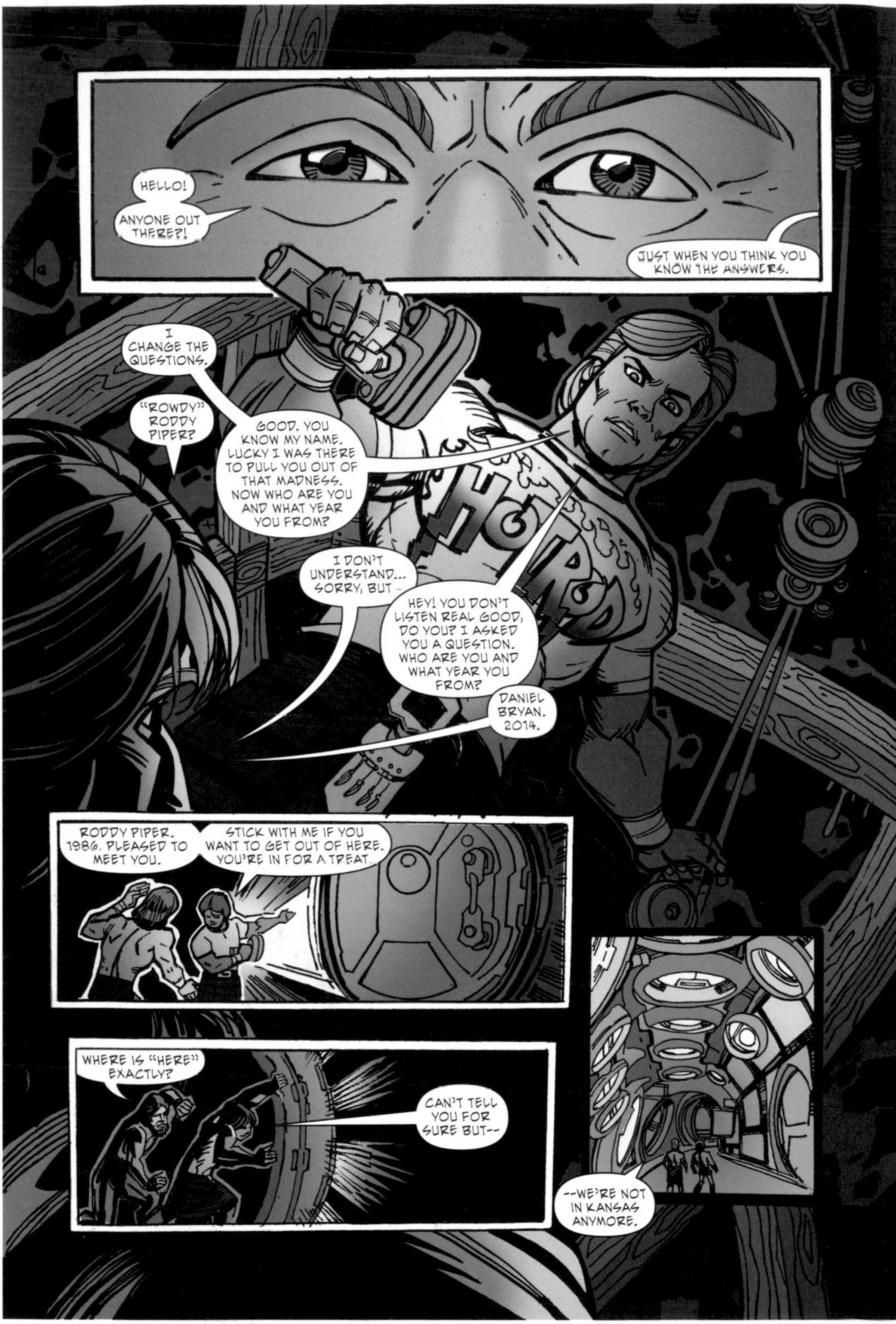
HELLO!
ANYONE OUT THERE?!
JUST WHEN YOU THINK YOU KNOW THE ANSWERS,
I CHANGE THE QUESTIONS.
"ROWDY" RODDY PIPER?
GOOD. YOU KNOW MY NAME. LUCKY I WAS THERE TO PULL YOU OUT OF THAT MADNESS. NOW WHO ARE YOU AND WHAT YEAR YOU FROM?
I DON'T UNDERSTAND... SORRY, BUT -
HEY! YOU DON'T LISTEN REAL GOOD, DO YOU? I ASKED YOU A QUESTION. WHO ARE YOU AND WHAT YEAR YOU FROM?
DANIEL BRYAN. 2014.
RODDY PIPER. 1986. PLEASED TO MEET YOU.
STICK WITH ME IF YOU WANT TO GET OUT OF HERE. YOU'RE IN FOR A TREAT.
WHERE IS "HERE" EXACTLY?
CAN'T TELL YOU FOR SURE BUT--
--WE'RE NOT IN KANSAS ANYMORE.

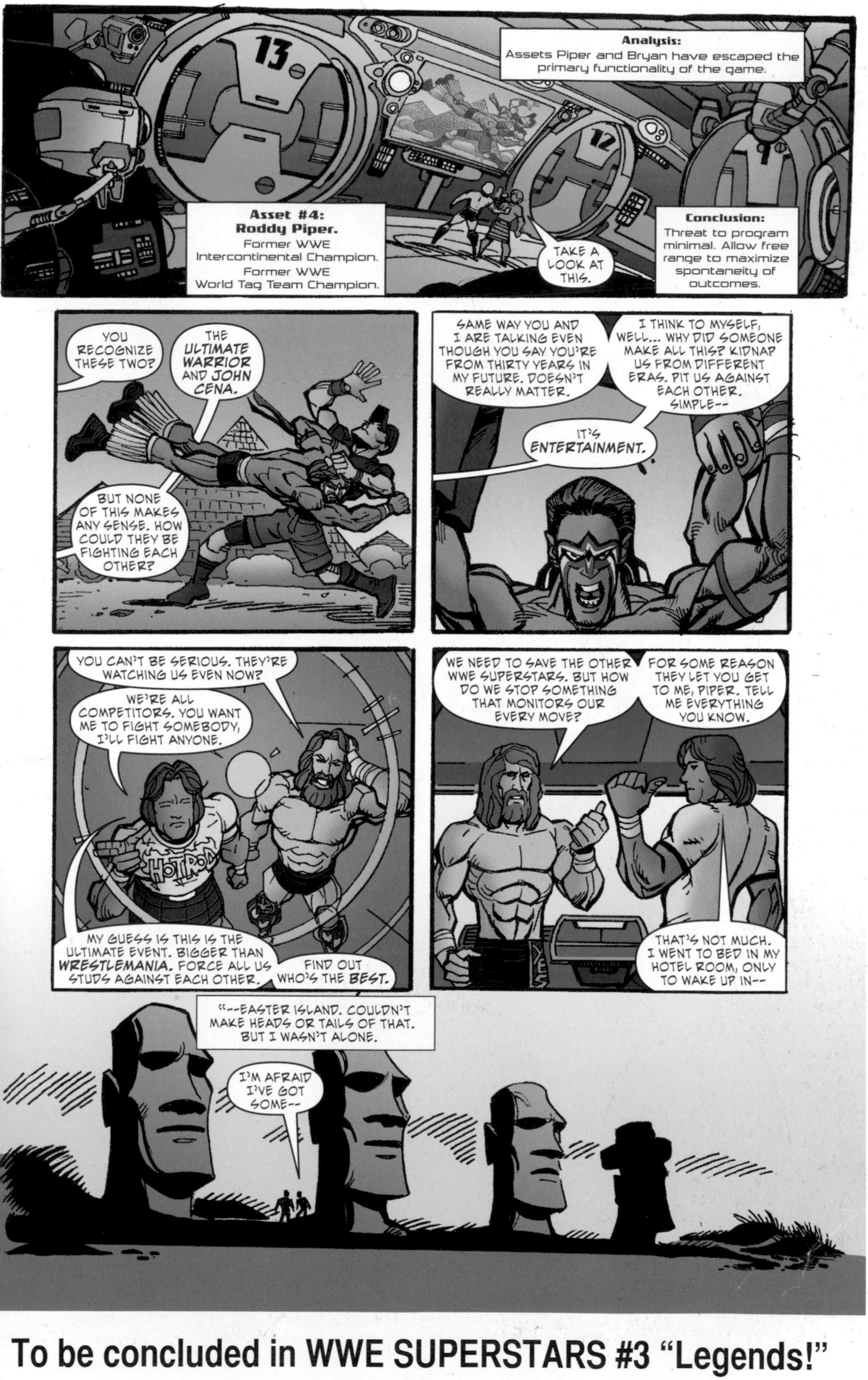

Analysis:
Assets Piper and Bryan have escaped the primary functionality of the game.
Asset #4:
Roddy Piper.
Former WWE Intercontinental Champion.
Former WWE World Tag Team Champion.
TAKE A LOOK AT THIS.
Conclusion:
Threat to program minimal. Allow free range to maximize spontaneity of outcomes.
YOU RECOGNIZE THESE TWO?
THE ULTIMATE WARRIOR AND JOHN CENA.
BUT NONE OF THIS MAKES ANY SENSE. HOW COULD THEY BE FIGHTING EACH OTHER?
SAME WAY YOU AND I ARE TALKING EVEN THOUGH YOU SAY YOU'RE FROM THIRTY YEARS IN MY FUTURE. DOESN'T REALLY MATTER.
I THINK TO MYSELF, WELL... WHY DID SOMEONE MAKE ALL THIS? KIDNAP US FROM DIFFERENT ERAS. PIT US AGAINST EACH OTHER. SIMPLE--
IT'S ENTERTAINMENT.
YOU CAN'T BE SERIOUS. THEY'RE WATCHING US EVEN NOW?
WE'RE ALL COMPETITORS. YOU WANT ME TO FIGHT SOMEBODY, I'LL FIGHT ANYONE.
MY GUESS IS THIS IS THE ULTIMATE EVENT. BIGGER THAN WRESTLEMANIA. FORCE ALL US STUDS AGAINST EACH OTHER.
FIND OUT WHO'S THE BEST.
WE NEED TO SAVE THE OTHER WWE SUPERSTARS. BUT HOW DO WE STOP SOMETHING THAT MONITORS OUR EVERY MOVE?
FOR SOME REASON THEY LET YOU GET TO ME, PIPER. TELL ME EVERYTHING YOU KNOW.
THAT'S NOT MUCH. I WENT TO BED IN MY HOTEL ROOM, ONLY TO WAKE UP IN--
"--EASTER ISLAND. COULDN'T MAKE HEADS OR TAILS OF THAT. BUT I WASN'T ALONE.
I'M AFRAID I'VE GOT SOME--

To be concluded in WWE SUPERSTARS #3 "Legends!"